THE FOLGER LIBRARY SHAKESPEARE

Designed to make Shakespeare's classic plays available to the general reader, each edition contains a reliable text with modernized spelling and punctuation, scene-by-scene plot summaries, and explanatory notes clarifying obscure and obsolete expressions. An interpretive essay and accounts of Shakespeare's life and theater form an instructive preface to each play.

Louis B. Wright, General Editor, was the Director of the Folger Shakespeare Library from 1948 until his retirement in 1968. He is the author of *Middle-Class Culture in Elizabethan England, Religion and Empire, Shakespeare for Everyman,* and many other books and essays on the history and literature of the Tudor and Stuart periods.

Virginia Lamar, Assistant Editor, served as research assistant to the Director and Executive Secretary of the Folger Shakespeare Library from 1946 until her death in 1968. She is the author of *English Dress in the Age of Shakespeare* and *Travel and Roads in England,* and coeditor of William Strachey's *Historie of Travell into Virginia Britania.*

The Folger Shakespeare Library

The Folger Shakespeare Library in Washington, D.C., a research institute founded and endowed by Henry Clay Folger and administered by the Trustees of Amherst College, contains the world's largest collection of Shakespeareana. Although the Folger Library's primary purpose is to encourage advanced research in history and literature, it has continually exhibited a profound concern in stimulating a popular interest in the Elizabethan period.

GENERAL EDITOR

LOUIS B. WRIGHT

Director, Folger Shakespeare Library, 1948–1968

ASSISTANT EDITOR

VIRGINIA A. LaMAR

Executive Secretary, Folger Shakespeare Library, 1946–1968

THE LIFE OF

KING HENRY THE FIFTH

by

WILLIAM SHAKESPEARE

WASHINGTON SQUARE PRESS
PUBLISHED BY POCKET BOOKS
New York   London   Toronto   Sydney   Tokyo   Singapore

WSP

A Washington Square Press Publication of
POCKET BOOKS, a division of Simon & Schuster Inc.
1230 Avenue of the Americas, New York, NY 10020

Copyright © 1960 by Simon & Schuster Inc.

ISBN: 0-671-72718-4

First Pocket Books printing September 1960

20 19 18 17 16 15 14

WASHINGTON SQUARE PRESS and WSP colophon are registered trademarks of Simon & Schuster Inc.

Printed in the U.S.A.

Preface

This edition of *Henry the Fifth* is designed to make available a readable text of one of Shakespeare's most popular plays. In the centuries since Shakespeare many changes have occurred in the meanings of words, and some clarification of Shakespeare's vocabulary may be helpful. To provide the reader with necessary notes in the most accessible format, we have placed them on the pages facing the text that they explain. We have tried to make these notes as brief and simple as possible. Preliminary to the text we have also included a brief statement of essential information about Shakespeare and his stage. Readers desiring more detailed information should refer to the books suggested in the references, and if still further information is needed, the bibliographies in those books will provide the necessary clues to the literature of the subject.

The early texts of all of Shakespeare's plays provide only inadequate stage directions, and it is conventional for modern editors to add many that clarify the action. Such additions, and additions to entrances, are placed in square brackets.

All illustrations are from material in the Folger Library collections.

L. B. W.
V. A. L.

October 15, 1959

Mirror of Kingship

When Shakespeare presented King Henry V to London audiences in the spring or summer of 1599 in a pageant-like play, he showed them a hero-king long established in the heroic tradition and one already popular on the stage. A shrewd appraiser of public taste, as always, Shakespeare took advantage of the swelling patriotism of the moment. When *Henry V* opened in London, England once more faced the prospect of war. The Irish had rebelled under Tyrone and had administered a stinging defeat to English troops. Now the Earl of Essex was ready to lead a punitive expedition against the troublesome Irish and conquer them once and for all. With a great concourse of people following and applauding him and his train, the noble Earl, a dashing character and the favorite of the Queen, marched out of London on March 27, 1599, bound for Ireland, and, as he and the populace believed, for victory and honor. That he would return defeated and disgraced in September was as yet a secret wrapped in the mists of Ireland.

No subject better than the deeds of King Henry V could have been chosen for the opening of the season in 1599, for Englishmen were enormously interested in the strength that he had brought to the Crown and the glory that he had won. By the end of the sixteenth century England was no longer the weak and puny country that it had been at the end of the Wars of the Roses, when Richard III had died at Bosworth Field and Henry Tudor had snatched his crown and made himself Henry VII. The country had grown strong under the Tudors and had taken its place as a world power under the greatest of them all, Elizabeth the Queen, Gloriana of the poets. Just eleven years before *Henry V* opened, England had defeated Spain, the mightiest power in the world, and had sent reeling home such galleons as survived from the vast invading Armada. Small wonder that Englishmen thrilled at the deeds of national heroes, present or past.

The reign of Elizabeth, especially the last two decades, saw an enormous interest in history and in historical plays. Felix Schelling, in his history of Elizabethan drama, has estimated that something like 220 plays during the Elizabethan period were drawn from the chronicles of British history, and that approximately half of these plays have survived. From 1588 to 1605, "more than a fifth of all contemporary plays" had for their themes some episode of British history. King John appeared in at least six plays, Henry V and Edward III in seven, Richard III in eight, and Henry VI was a character in at least ten. Of Shakespeare's plays, thirteen, or about one-third, used British history, or legend that passed for history, as their theme. The appetite for historical reading matter was enormous and the

greatest poets and writers set out to satisfy this
interest.

Shakespeare had already achieved success in historical drama before *Henry V* was written. Indeed,
this play was a sequel promised the public who had
taken the two parts of *Henry IV* to its heart. At the
end of *Henry IV (Part 2)*, Prince Hal succeeds to
the throne and renounces Falstaff and his madcap
cronies. The Epilogue, however, promises that the
historical drama will continue with another play in
which Falstaff will also appear: "If you be not too
much cloyed with fat meat, our humble author will
continue his story, with Sir John in it, and make
you merry with fair Katherine of France; where, for
anything I know, Falstaff shall die of a sweat, unless already 'a be killed with your hard opinions."
Henry V followed according to promise, but Falstaff was not in it. Shakespeare changed his plan
and killed Falstaff off stage near the beginning of
the play. Perhaps he felt that the fat knight would
steal too many of the scenes in a play which sought
to focus interest upon the King himself.

For *Henry V* is primarily concerned with the hero-
king, with the prowess that such a king displays,
with the glory that comes to England through the
king's exploits, and with the problem of kingship
as such. Given the spirit of the times, any drum-and-
trumpet play would have attracted attention, but
Shakespeare wrote something more and something
deeper. His is a drama that breathes the spirit of
the new nationalism that suffused England; though

it is set in a previous age, it reflects with striking immediacy the attitudes and concepts of his own period. While the spectators applauded Henry V on the "vasty fields of France," they were also conscious of their own heroic Queen and they may have remembered how, eleven years before, she had ridden her charger before the troops drawn up at Tilbury to repulse the Spanish invaders.

Henry V was a hero who appealed to the Elizabethans. In the face of heavy odds he had won a great victory against a traditional enemy. He was a strong king, who united the country behind him and showed to everyone, at home and abroad, that he would brook neither disorder within his borders nor encroachments from without. Furthermore, Shakespeare made him both God-fearing and just, qualities that the English believed their Queen possessed. She was supreme head of the church and she was the ultimate arbiter of a justice that the English had come to prize as one of their most priceless legacies. Shakespeare makes of Henry the ideal sovereign, or as the Chorus to Act II expresses it, "the mirror of all Christian kings."

The problem of kingship and the nature of the office interested the Renaissance generally and the Elizabethans particularly. England had suffered from weak rulers during the Wars of the Roses until, in the end, the rise of the Tudors had brought stability and prosperity. Works of history, plays, and poems, as well as popular legend and story, kept alive the memory of the chaotic conditions that existed before the accession of Henry Tudor, and no Englishman wanted a return of civil strife. Strength and justice were the qualities most admired in a sovereign, and the majority of Englishmen agreed that the Tudors supplied both. Queen Elizabeth had shrewdly capitalized upon her subjects' yearning for stability, and she managed to identify herself so completely with the public weal that Englishmen could hardly think of a form of government or a sovereign more benign.

But lurking in the back of every Englishman's head was the thought of what might happen when the Queen was no more, for the succession was in doubt, and the fear of civil commotion was a ghost that could not be laid. Far more depended upon the succession than depends upon the outcome of the most critical election today. All of these facts gave special point to the histories of previous English sovereigns and are a further explanation of the popular interest in history plays. In Shakespeare's *Richard II* the public could see the evils that come upon the commonwealth when a king is weak and vacillating; in the three plays concerning Henry IV and Henry V they could see and appreciate the benefits of a strong dynasty. There is no question that audiences would equate for themselves the qualities of the great Plantagenets with those of the great Tudors. Consequently, for the spectators in 1599 *Henry V* was timely, topical, and of consuming interest.

Victorian and modern critics at times have found

much fault with *Henry V*. To some, the reversal of the madcap qualities of Prince Hal and his conversion into a sedate, pious, and business-like ruler once he has succeeded to the throne are unrealistic and unconvincing. To others, the new King's hard and callous rejection of his old pot-companion Falstaff is too brutal to accept. To still others, the King's undertaking of a bloody campaign of aggression in France is proof of nothing except territorial greed. And lastly, to many the play has appeared lacking in structure, a sequence of poorly related scenes.

All of these criticisms are beside the point when one considers Shakespeare's purpose, the interpretation that he intended, and the attitude of the Elizabethans. We must remember that sixteenth-century concepts of character, of the responsibilities and obligations of a king, of war and peace—even of dramatic structure—differed radically from those possessed by the Victorians or by us.

For Henry to have retained the companionship of Falstaff after he had become king would have violated every canon of propriety understood by the Elizabethans. The King might have retained the services of a clown but not the fellowship of a clownish soldier and roistering reprobate. Having assumed the obligations of the crown, Henry had to put aside the frivolities of his irresponsible youth. There was a divinity that hedged a crown, and comic rascality had no place near it. Falstaff had to go. Sentimentalists who shed tears over Falstaff's discomfiture forget that to an Elizabethan the King's action in dismissing Falstaff at the end of *Henry IV, Part II,* was both proper and just. Though he forbade Falstaff to come within ten miles of the royal presence, he commanded that he be given a "competence of life"—in short, a pension. When the new play of *Henry V* opens, the King is no longer encumbered with cronies unbecoming a ruler. He is the very picture of an upright king.

The justification for Shakespeare's attribution of religious piety to Henry is found in his sources as well as in the dramatist's own purpose. He wanted to portray the perfect ruler, the character that he proposed to give to the chief protagonist in his play, and the perfect ruler was the spiritual as well as the temporal leader of his people. That was what Elizabethans understood. Their Queen was at pains to let nobody forget that she was supreme head of the church. That was the role that her father, Henry VIII, had assumed, and she had no choice, even if she had wished otherwise, than to maintain that position, for the stability of her throne depended upon her supremacy in spiritual as well as political affairs. Henry V is not the pious hypocrite that some unhistorical critics have made him; instead he is a sovereign mindful of his spiritual duties.

To an Elizabethan, Henry's undertaking the conquest of France was not naked aggression but the assertion of a legal right which it was his duty to enforce even at the expense of war. That is the point of the long passages at the beginning of the play in which the Archbishop of Canterbury expounds the fine points of the law of succession. Henry V—as well as Shakespeare—wants to make clear the legality of his claims and the justice of his cause. Whether we approve or not, Shakespeare's audience was convinced and they approved his actions. War was a part of life in the sixteenth century and few if any dreamed of banishing war as an instrument for enforcing national policies.

Although Shakespeare at times could be careless and forgetful of minor details, he was too skillful a dramatist merely to fling together a series of episodic scenes in a military pageant as some critics have implied. It is true that some of the comic scenes have little relation to the main plot, and occasionally there is evidence of hasty reworking of the material, as in Act IV, Scene vii, where no provision is made for Gower's exit, though the King talks about him as if he had left the stage. But *Henry V* is not a play without a plan. It must be interpreted as part of a trilogy that began with *Henry IV, Part I*, as the final element in a dramatic epic of the reigns of these strong Plantagenet kings.

Since Shakespeare was writing an epic of history, he was circumscribed by the known facts in what he could do. Although he could telescope the action and let a chorus account for the passage of years, he could not take too much poetic license with the actual deeds of the English in France or with the results of the war.

To provide information that the stage could not

portray and to bring his historical episodes into focus, he employed the technique of a Prologue, an explanatory chorus before each act, and a concluding chorus that serves as an Epilogue. These elements deserve careful study for the information that they provide, not only about the action itself, but about Shakespeare's intentions. That the play has been an enduring success since its first performance is an indication that it is something more than a mere military pageant. It is Shakespeare's epic interpretation on the stage of the career of a national hero, and the poetry that Shakespeare wrote into this play has appealed to Englishmen in every national crisis from that day to this.

SOURCES AND STAGE HISTORY

As was his usual custom in writing a play on British history, Shakespeare turned to Raphael Holinshed's *Chronicles of England, Scotland, and Ireland* (1577–87) for the information, and sometimes the phraseology, that he wanted. But he did not stop with Holinshed. He consulted Edward Hall's *The Union of the Two Noble and Illustrate Families, of Lancaster and York* (1548), which Holinshed himself had used as a source, and he apparently knew an older play on the same subject, *The Famous Victories of Henry V* (ca. 1586–87). In addition, some editors find traces of other works bearing on Shakespeare's theme. For example, Dover Wilson thinks Shakespeare knew a Latin life of Henry V, written by his chaplain, entitled *Henrici Quinti, Angliae Regis Gesta*, and others have found an echo of a second Latin biography, *Vita et Gesta Henrici Quinti*, but it is doubtful whether Shakespeare went to work like a college professor to find bits and pieces when he had all that he needed in Hall and Holinshed; these English histories supplied ample raw material. At times he merely cast into blank verse the prose of Holinshed or Hall, as in the opening scenes of the play where the Archbishop of Canterbury discusses the Salic law.

The first printed version of *Henry V*, the corrupt quarto of 1600, announced on the title page that it had "been sundry times played by the right honorable the Lord Chamberlain his servants," that is to say, by Shakespeare's company of players. The date of the first performance is fixed within fairly definite limits by a flattering allusion of the Chorus of Act V to the Earl of Essex's expedition to Ireland, which set out from London on March 27, 1599. Since the venture failed and Essex returned in disgrace in September of the same year, the play must have been acted before that date. The reference in the Prologue to "this wooden O" has been taken to mean the Globe playhouse, but it is not certain precisely when in 1599 the Globe was completed. The place of first performance may have been another of the public theatres.

Although *Henry V* was apparently a popular play, surviving records of its early stage history are scanty. We know that it was performed at Court before

King James on January 7, 1605, as part of the
Christmas holiday festivities. During the Restoration
it was revived and Samuel Pepys saw Thomas Betterton play the King at Lincoln's Inn Fields on July
6, 1668, but there is little evidence of other performances of the play until well into the eighteenth
century. Aaron Hill borrowed from Shakespeare for
a play of his own on the same theme, but by 1735
Shakespeare's text was restored to the theatre and
thenceforth *Henry V* was seen at regular intervals
on the English stage. It was popular at both Drury
Lane and Covent Garden and many of the most
noted actors of the eighteenth, nineteenth, and
twentieth centuries have played in it. David Garrick
chose to serve as Prologue and Chorus on several
occasions, an indication of the importance that he
attached to that role. Perhaps the strangest recorded
performance of *Henry V* was that at Stratford-upon-
Avon on Shakespeare's birthday, 1921, with an all-
woman cast in which Marie Slade played the King.

The mid-nineteenth-century theatre often at-
tempted naturalistic realism in staging the play, a
mistake that saw some fantastic stage sets as producers tried to remedy the inadequacies that Shakespeare's Prologue had described. Some of the spec-
tacles provided dioramas of Henry's ships moving
from Southampton to Harfleur and of great battle
scenes. It remained, however, for Sir Laurence
Olivier to weld poetry and scenic effects into a
convincing unity in the motion-picture version of
Henry V, first seen in England in November 1944.

This version of the play has had an enormous popularity on both sides of the Atlantic and fifteen years after its première it is still being seen in British and American theatres.

THE TEXT

The text of *Henry V* printed in the First Folio of 1623 is the basis of all modern editions of the play. Although this text is reasonably free from mislineations, misspellings, and other mistakes, some passages require emendation to make proper sense, and editors have made some use of the quarto versions in an effort to arrive at Shakespeare's meaning. The First Quarto, printed in 1600 by Thomas Creede for Thomas Millington and John Busby, is an abbreviated and corrupt text, shorter by about two thousand lines than the Folio text. Suggestions as to the origin of this quarto version include a text put together from memory by one or more of the actors, and a text taken down by shorthand. A suggestion has also been made that it was a stage version cut for a provincial performance. In any case it is a perversion of the text that was used for the Folio printing, presumably an acceptable playhouse manuscript.

Two other quarto versions appeared before the publication of the First Folio, the Second Quarto of 1602 and the Third Quarto of 1619, but these are not independent versions and merely reprint with some corrections the text of the First Quarto.

As early as 1598 Shakespeare was so well known as a literary and dramatic craftsman that Francis Meres, in his *Palladis Tamia: Wits Treasury*, referred in flattering terms to him as "mellifluous and honey-tongued Shakespeare," famous for his *Venus and Adonis*, his *Lucrece*, and "his sugared sonnets," which were circulating "among his private friends." Meres observes further that "as Plautus and Seneca are accounted the best for comedy and tragedy among the Latins, so Shakespeare among the English is the most excellent in both kinds for the stage," and he mentions a dozen plays that had made a name for Shakespeare. He concludes with the remark "that the Muses would speak with Shakespeare's fine filed phrase if they would speak English."

To those acquainted with the history of the Elizabethan and Jacobean periods, it is incredible that anyone should be so naïve or ignorant as to doubt the reality of Shakespeare as the author of the plays that bear his name. Yet so much nonsense has been written about other "candidates" for the plays that it is well to remind readers that no credible evidence that would stand up in a court of law has ever been adduced to prove either that Shakespeare did not write his plays or that anyone else wrote them. All the theories offered for the authorship of Francis Bacon, the Earl of Derby, the Earl of Oxford, the Earl of Hertford, Christopher Marlowe, and a score of other candidates are mere conjectures spun from the active imaginations of persons who confuse hypothesis and conjecture with evidence.

As Meres' statement of 1598 indicates, Shakespeare was already a popular playwright whose name carried weight at the box office. The obvious reputation of Shakespeare as early as 1598 makes the effort to prove him a myth one of the most absurd in the history of human perversity.

The anti-Shakespeareans talk darkly about a plot of vested interests to maintain the authorship of Shakespeare. Nobody has any vested interest in Shakespeare, but every scholar is interested in the truth and in the quality of evidence advanced by special pleaders who set forth hypotheses in place of facts.

The anti-Shakespeareans base their arguments upon a few simple premises, all of them false. These false premises are that Shakespeare was an unlettered yokel without any schooling, that nothing is known about Shakespeare, and that only a noble lord or the equivalent in background could have written the plays. The facts are that more is known about Shakespeare than about most dramatists of his day, that he had a very good education, acquired in the Stratford Grammar School, that the plays show no evidence of profound book learning, and that the knowledge of kings and courts evident in the plays is no greater than any intelligent young man could have picked up at second hand. Most anti-Shakespeareans are naïve and betray an obvious snobbery. The author of their favorite plays, they imply, must have had a college diploma framed and hung on his study wall like the one in their dentist's office, and obviously so great a writer must have had a title or some equally significant evidence of exalted social background. They forget that genius has a way of cropping up in unexpected places and that none of the great creative writers of the world got his inspiration in a college or university course.

William Shakespeare was the son of John Shakespeare of Stratford-upon-Avon, a substantial citizen of that small but busy market town in the center of the rich agricultural county of Warwick. John Shakespeare kept a shop, what we would call a general store; he dealt in wool and other produce and gradually acquired property. As a youth, John Shakespeare had learned the trade of glover and leather worker. There is no contemporary evidence that the elder Shakespeare was a butcher, though the anti-Shakespeareans like to talk about the ignorant "butcher's boy of Stratford." Their only evidence is a statement by gossipy John Aubrey, more than a century after William Shakespeare's birth, that young William followed his father's trade, and when he killed a calf, "he would do it in a high style and make a speech." We would like to believe the story true, but Aubrey is not a very credible witness.

John Shakespeare probably continued to operate a farm at Snitterfield that his father had leased. He married Mary Arden, daughter of his father's landlord, a man of some property. The third of their eight children was William, baptized on April 26,

1564, and probably born three days before. At least, it is conventional to celebrate April 23 as his birthday.

The Stratford records give considerable information about John Shakespeare. We know that he held several municipal offices including those of alderman and mayor. In 1580 he was in some sort of legal difficulty and was fined for neglecting a summons of the Court of Queen's Bench requiring him to appear at Westminster and be bound over to keep the peace.

As a citizen and alderman of Stratford, John Shakespeare was entitled to send his son to the grammar school free. Though the records are lost, there can be no reason to doubt that this is where young William received his education. As any student of the period knows, the grammar schools provided the basic education in Latin learning and literature. The Elizabethan grammar school is not to be confused with modern grammar schools. Many cultivated men of the day received all their formal education in the grammar schools. At the universities in this period a student would have received little training that would have inspired him to be a creative writer. At Stratford young Shakespeare would have acquired a familiarity with Latin and some little knowledge of Greek. He would have read Latin authors and become acquainted with the plays of Plautus and Terence. Undoubtedly, in this period of his life he received that stimulation to read and explore for himself the world of ancient and modern history which he later utilized in his plays. The youngster who does not acquire this type of intellectual curiosity *before* college days rarely develops as a result of a college course the kind of mind Shakespeare demonstrated. His learning in books was anything but profound, but he clearly had the probing curiosity that sent him in search of information, and he had a keenness in the observation of nature and of humankind that finds reflection in his poetry.

There is little documentation for Shakespeare's boyhood. There is little reason why there should be. Nobody knew that he was going to be a dramatist about whom any scrap of information would be prized in the centuries to come. He was merely an active and vigorous youth of Stratford, perhaps assisting his father in his business, and no Boswell bothered to write down facts about him. The most important record that we have is a marriage license issued by the Bishop of Worcester on November 28, 1582, to permit William Shakespeare to marry Anne Hathaway, seven or eight years his senior; furthermore, the Bishop permitted the marriage after reading the banns only once instead of three times, evidence of the desire for haste. The need was explained on May 26, 1583, when the christening of Susanna, daughter of William and Anne Shakespeare, was recorded at Stratford. Two years later, on February 2, 1585, the records show the birth of twins to the Shakespeares, a boy and a girl who were christened Hamnet and Judith.

What William Shakespeare was doing in Stratford during the early years of his married life, or when he went to London, we do not know. It has been conjectured that he tried his hand at school-teaching, but that is a mere guess. There is a legend that he left Stratford to escape a charge of poaching in the park of Sir Thomas Lucy of Charlecote, but there is no proof of this. There is also a legend that when first he came to London, he earned his living by holding horses outside a playhouse and presently was given employment inside, but there is nothing better than eighteenth-century hearsay for this. How Shakespeare broke into the London theatres as a dramatist and actor we do not know. But lack of information is not surprising, for Elizabethans did not write their autobiographies, and we know even less about the lives of many writers and some men of affairs than we know about Shakespeare. By 1592 he was so well established and popular that he incurred the envy of the dramatist and pamphleteer Robert Greene, who referred to him as an "upstart crow . . . in his own conceit the only Shake-scene in a country." From this time onward, contemporary allusions and references in legal documents enable the scholar to chart Shakespeare's career with greater accuracy than is possible with most other Elizabethan dramatists.

By 1594 Shakespeare was a member of the company of actors known as the Lord Chamberlain's Men. After the accession of James I, in 1603, the company would have the sovereign for their patron and would be known as the King's Men. During the period of its greatest prosperity, this company would have as its principal theatres the Globe and the Blackfriars. Shakespeare was both an actor and a shareholder in the company. Tradition has assigned him such acting roles as Adam in *As You Like It* and the Ghost in *Hamlet,* a modest place on the stage that suggests that he may have had other duties in the management of the company. Such conclusions, however, are based on surmise.

What we do know is that his plays were popular and that he was highly successful in his vocation. His first play may have been *The Comedy of Errors,* acted perhaps in 1591. Certainly this was one of his earliest plays. The three parts of *Henry VI* were acted sometime between 1590 and 1592. Critics are not in agreement about precisely how much Shakespeare wrote of these three plays. *Richard III* probably dates from 1593. With this play Shakespeare captured the imagination of Elizabethan audiences, then enormously interested in historical plays. With *Richard III* Shakespeare also gave an interpretation pleasing to the Tudors of the rise to power of the grandfather of Queen Elizabeth. From this time onward, Shakespeare's plays followed on the stage in rapid succession: *Titus Andronicus, The Taming of the Shrew, The Two Gentlemen of Verona, Love's Labour's Lost, Romeo and Juliet, Richard II, A Midsummer Night's Dream, King John, The Merchant of Venice, Henry IV (Parts 1 and 2), Much Ado About Nothing, Henry V, Julius Cæsar, As You Like It, Twelfth Night, Hamlet, The Merry Wives of Windsor, All's Well That Ends Well, Measure for Measure, Othello, King Lear,* and nine others that followed before Shakespeare retired completely, about 1613.

In the course of his career in London, he made enough money to enable him to retire to Stratford with a competence. His purchase on May 4, 1597, of New Place, then the second-largest dwelling in Stratford, a "pretty house of brick and timber," with a handsome garden, indicates his increasing prosperity. There his wife and children lived while he busied himself in the London theatres. The summer before he acquired New Place, his life was darkened by the death of his only son, Hamnet, a child of eleven. In May, 1602, Shakespeare purchased one hundred and seven acres of fertile farmland near Stratford and a few months later bought a cottage and garden across the alley from New Place. About 1611, he seems to have returned permanently to Stratford, for the next year a legal document refers to him as "William Shakespeare of Stratford-upon-Avon . . . gentleman." To achieve the desired appellation of gentleman, William Shakespeare had seen to it that the College of Heralds in 1596 granted his father a coat of arms. In one step he thus became a second-generation gentleman.

Shakespeare's daughter Susanna made a good match in 1607 with Dr. John Hall, a prominent and prosperous Stratford physician. His second daughter, Judith, did not marry until she was thirty-two years old, and then, under somewhat scandalous circumstances, she married Thomas Quiney, a Stratford vintner. On March 25, 1616, Shakespeare made his will, bequeathing his landed property to Susanna, £300 to Judith, certain sums to other relatives, and his second-best bed to his wife, Anne. Much has been made of the second-best bed, but the legacy probably indicates only that Anne liked that particular bed. Shakespeare, following the practice of the time, may have already arranged with Susanna for his wife's care. Finally, on April 23, 1616, the anniversary of his birth, William Shakespeare died, and he was buried on April 25 within the chancel of Trinity Church, as befitted an honored citizen. On August 6, 1623, a few months before the publication of the collected edition of Shakespeare's plays, Anne Shakespeare joined her husband in death.

THE PUBLICATION OF HIS PLAYS

During his lifetime Shakespeare made no effort to publish any of his plays, though eighteen appeared in print in single-play editions known as quartos. Some of these are corrupt versions known as "bad quartos." No quarto, so far as is known, had the author's approval. Plays were not considered "literature" any more than most radio and television scripts today are considered literature. Dramatists sold their plays outright to the theatrical companies and it was usually considered in the company's interest to keep plays from getting into print. To achieve a reputation as a man of letters, Shakespeare wrote his *Sonnets* and his narrative poems, *Venus and Adonis* and *The Rape of Lucrece*, but he probably never dreamed that his plays would establish his reputation as a literary genius. Only Ben Jonson, a man known for his colossal conceit, had the crust to call his plays *Works,* as he did when he published an edition in 1616. But men laughed at Ben Jonson.

After Shakespeare's death, two of his old colleagues in the King's Men, John Heminges and Henry Condell, decided that it would be a good thing to print, in more accurate versions than were then available, the plays already published and eighteen additional plays not previously published in quarto. In 1623 appeared *Mr. William Shakespeares Comedies, Histories, & Tragedies. Published according to the True Originall Copies. London. Printed by Isaac Iaggard and Ed. Blount.* This was the famous First Folio, a work that had the authority of Shakespeare's associates. The only play commonly attributed to Shakespeare that was omitted in the First Folio was *Pericles.* In their preface, "To the great Variety of Readers," Heminges and Condell state that whereas "you were abused with diverse stolen and surreptitious copies, maimed and deformed by the frauds and stealths of injurious impostors that exposed them, even those are now offered to your view cured and perfect of their limbs; and all the rest, absolute in their numbers, as he conceived them." What they used for printer's copy is one of the vexed problems of scholarship, and skilled bibliographers have devoted years of study to the question of the relation of the "copy" for the First Folio to Shakespeare's manuscripts. In some cases it is clear that the editors corrected printed quarto versions of the plays, probably by comparison with playhouse scripts. Whether these scripts were in Shakespeare's autograph is anybody's guess. No manuscript of any play in Shakespeare's handwriting has survived. Indeed, very few play manuscripts from this period by any author are extant. The Tudor and Stuart periods had not yet learned to prize autographs and authors' original manuscripts.

Since the First Folio contains eighteen plays not previously printed, it is the only source for these. For the other eighteen, which had appeared in quarto versions, the First Folio also has the authority of an edition prepared and overseen by Shakespeare's colleagues and professional associates. But since editorial standards in 1623 were far from strict, and Heminges and Condell were actors rather than editors by profession, the texts are sometimes careless. The printing and proofreading of the First Folio also left much to be desired, and some garbled passages have to be corrected and emended. The "good quarto" texts have to be taken into account in preparing a modern edition.

Because of the great popularity of Shakespeare through the centuries, the First Folio has become a prized book, but it is not a very rare one, for it is estimated that 238 copies are extant. The Folger Shakespeare Library in Washington, D.C., has seventy-nine copies of the First Folio, collected by the founder, Henry Clay Folger, who believed that a collation of as many texts as possible would reveal significant facts about the text of Shakespeare's plays. Dr. Charlton Hinman, using an ingenious machine of his own invention for mechanical collating, has made many discoveries that throw light on Shakespeare's text and on printing practices of the day.

The probability is that the First Folio of 1623 had an edition of between 1,000 and 1,250 copies. It is believed that it sold for £1, which made it an expensive book, for £1 in 1623 was equivalent to something between $40 and $50 in modern purchasing power.

During the seventeenth century, Shakespeare was sufficiently popular to warrant three later editions in folio size, the Second Folio of 1632, the Third Folio of 1663–1664, and the Fourth Folio of 1685. The Third Folio added six other plays ascribed to Shakespeare, but these are apocryphal.

THE SHAKESPEAREAN THEATRE

The theatres in which Shakespeare's plays were performed were vastly different from those we know today. The stage was a platform that jutted out into the area now occupied by the first rows of seats on the main floor, what is called the "orchestra" in America and the "pit" in England. This platform had no curtain to come down at the ends of acts and scenes. And although simple stage properties were available, the Elizabethan theatre lacked both the machinery and the elaborate movable scenery of the modern theatre. In the rear of the platform stage was a curtained area that could be used as an inner room, a tomb, or any such scene that might be required. A balcony above this inner room, and perhaps balconies on the sides of the stage, could represent the upper deck of a ship, the entry to Juliet's room, or a prison window. A trap door in the stage provided an entrance for ghosts and devils from the nether regions, and a similar trap in the canopied structure over the stage, known as the "heavens," made it possible to let down angels on a rope. These primitive stage arrangements help to account for many elements in Elizabethan plays. For example, since there was no curtain, the dramatist frequently felt the necessity of writing into his play action to clear the stage at the ends of acts and scenes. The funeral march at the end of *Hamlet* is not there merely for atmosphere; Shakespeare had to get the corpses off the stage. The lack of scenery also freed the dramatist from undue concern about the exact location of his sets, and the physical relation of his various settings to each other did not have to be worked out with the same precision as in the modern theatre.

Before London had buildings designed exclusively for theatrical entertainment, plays were given in inns and taverns. The characteristic inn of the period had an inner courtyard with rooms opening onto balconies overlooking the yard. Players could set up their temporary stages at one end of the yard and audiences could find seats on the balconies out of the weather. The poorer sort could stand or sit on the cobblestones in the yard, which was open to the sky. The first theatres followed this construction, and throughout the Elizabethan period the large public theatres had a yard in front of the stage open to the weather, with two or three tiers of covered balconies extending around the theatre. This physical structure again influenced the writing of plays. Because a dramatist wanted the actors to be heard, he frequently wrote into his play orations that could be delivered with declamatory effect. He also provided spectacle, buffoonery, and broad jests to keep the riotous groundlings in the yard entertained and quiet.

In another respect the Elizabethan theatre differed greatly from ours. It had no actresses. All women's roles were taken by boys, sometimes recruited from the boys' choirs of the London churches. Some of these youths acted their roles with great skill and the Elizabethans did not seem to be aware of any incongruity. The first actresses on the professional English stage appeared after the Restoration of Charles II, in 1660, when exiled Englishmen brought back from France practices of the French stage.

London in the Elizabethan period, as now, was the center of theatrical interest, though wandering actors from time to time traveled through the country performing in inns, halls, and the houses of the nobility. The first professional playhouse, called simply The Theatre, was erected by James Burbage, father of Shakespeare's colleague Richard Burbage, in 1576 on lands of the old Holywell Priory adjacent to Finsbury Fields, a playground and park area just north of the city walls. It had the advantage of being outside the city's jurisdiction and yet was near enough to be easily accessible. Soon after The Theatre was opened, another playhouse called The Curtain was erected in the same neighborhood. Both of these playhouses had open courtyards and were probably polygonal in shape.

About the time The Curtain opened, Richard Farrant, Master of the Children of the Chapel Royal at Windsor and of St. Paul's, conceived the idea of opening a "private" theatre in the old monastery buildings of the Blackfriars, not far from St. Paul's Cathedral in the heart of the city. This theatre was ostensibly to train the choirboys in plays for presentation at Court, but Farrant managed to present plays to paying audiences and achieved considerable success until aristocratic neighbors complained and had the theatre closed. This first Blackfriars Theatre was significant, however, because it popularized the boy actors in a professional way and it paved the way for a second theatre in the Blackfriars, which Shakespeare's company took over more than thirty years later. By the last years of the sixteenth century, London had at least six professional theatres, and still others were erected during the reign of James I.

The Globe Theatre, the playhouse that most people connect with Shakespeare, was erected early in 1599 on the Bankside, the area across the Thames from the city. Its construction had a dramatic beginning, for on the night of December 28, 1598, James Burbage's sons, Cuthbert and Richard, gathered together a crew who tore down the old theatre in Holywell and carted the timbers across the river to a site that they had chosen for a new playhouse. The reason for this clandestine operation was a row with the landowner over the lease to the Holywell property. The site chosen for the Globe was another playground outside of the city's jurisdiction, a region of somewhat unsavory character. Not far away was the Bear Garden, an amphitheatre devoted to the baiting of bears and bulls. This was also the region occupied by many houses of ill fame licensed by the Bishop of Winchester and the source of substantial revenue to him. But it was easily accessible either from London Bridge or by means of the cheap boats operated by the London watermen, and it had the great advantage of being beyond the authority of the Puritanical aldermen of London, who frowned on plays because they lured apprentices from work, filled their heads with improper ideas, and generally exerted a bad influence. The aldermen also complained that the crowds drawn together in the theatre helped to spread the plague.

The Globe was the handsomest theatre up to its time. It was a large building, apparently octagonal in shape and open like its predecessors to the sky in the center, but capable of seating a large audience in its covered balconies. To erect and operate the Globe, the Burbages organized a syndicate com-

posed of the leading members of the dramatic
company, of which Shakespeare was a member.
Since it was open to the weather and depended on
natural light, plays had to be given in the after-
noon. This caused no hardship in the long after-
noons of an English summer, but in the winter the
weather was a great handicap and discouraged all
except the hardiest. For that reason, in 1608 Shakespeare's company was glad to take over the lease
of the second Blackfriars Theatre, a substantial,
roomy hall reconstructed within the framework of
the old monastery building. This theatre was pro-
tected from the weather and its stage was artificial-
ly lighted by chandeliers of candles. This became
the winter playhouse for Shakespeare's company
and at once proved so popular that the congestion
of traffic created an embarrassing problem. Strin-
gent regulations had to be made for the movement
of coaches in the vicinity. Shakespeare's company
continued to use the Globe during the summer
months. In 1613 a squib fired from a cannon during
a performance of *Henry VIII* fell on the thatched
roof and the Globe burned to the ground. The
next year it was rebuilt.

London had other famous theatres. The Rose,
just west of the Globe, was built by Philip Henslowe, a semiliterate denizen of the Bankside, who
became one of the most important theatrical owners
and producers of the Tudor and Stuart periods.
What is more important for historians, he kept a
detailed account book, which provides much of our
information about theatrical history in his time.

Another famous theatre on the Bankside was the Swan, which a Dutch priest, Johannes de Witt, visited in 1596. The crude drawing of the stage which he made was copied by his friend Arend van Buchell; it is one of the important pieces of contemporary evidence for theatrical construction. Among the other theatres, the Fortune, north of the city, on Golding Lane, and the Red Bull, even farther away from the city, off St. John's Street, were the most popular. The Red Bull, much frequented by apprentices, favored sensational and sometimes rowdy plays.

The actors who kept all of these theatres going were organized into companies under the protection of some noble patron. Traditionally actors had enjoyed a low reputation. In some of the ordinances they were classed as vagrants; in the phraseology of the time, "rogues, vagabonds, sturdy beggars, and common players" were all listed together as undesirables. To escape penalties often meted out to these characters, organized groups of actors managed to gain the protection of various personages of high degree. In the later years of Elizabeth's reign, a group flourished under the name of the Queen's Men; another group had the protection of the Lord Admiral and were known as the Lord Admiral's Men. Edward Alleyn, son-in-law of Philip Henslowe, was the leading spirit in the Lord Admiral's Men. Besides the adult companies, troupes of boy actors from time to time also enjoyed considerable popularity. Among these were the Children of Paul's and the Children of the Chapel Royal.

The company with which Shakespeare had a long association had for its first patron Henry Carey, Lord Hunsdon, the Lord Chamberlain, and hence they were known as the Lord Chamberlain's Men. After the accession of James I, they became the King's Men. This company was the great rival of the Lord Admiral's Men, managed by Henslowe and Alleyn.

All was not easy for the players in Shakespeare's time, for the aldermen of London were always eager for an excuse to close up the Blackfriars and any other theatres in their jurisdiction. The theatres outside the jurisdiction of London were not immune from interference, for they might be shut up by order of the Privy Council for meddling in politics or for various other offenses, or they might be closed in time of plague lest they spread infection. During plague times, the actors usually went on tour and played the provinces wherever they could find an audience. Particularly frightening were the plagues of 1592–1594 and 1613 when the theatres closed and the players, like many other Londoners, had to take to the country.

Though players had a low social status, they enjoyed great popularity, and one of the favorite forms of entertainment at Court was the performance of plays. To be commanded to perform at Court conferred great prestige upon a company of players, and printers frequently noted that fact when they published plays. Several of Shakespeare's plays were performed before the sovereign, and Shakespeare himself undoubtedly acted in some of these plays.

REFERENCES FOR FURTHER READING

Many readers will want suggestions for further reading about Shakespeare and his times. The literature in this field is enormous but a few references will serve as guides to further study. A simple and useful little book is Gerald Sanders, *A Shakespeare Primer* (New York, 1950). *A Companion to Shakespeare Studies*, edited by Harley Granville-Barker and G. B. Harrison (Cambridge, Eng., 1934) is a valuable guide. More detailed but still not too voluminous to be confusing is Hazelton Spencer, *The Art and Life of William Shakespeare* (New York, 1940) which, like Sanders' handbook, contains a brief annotated list of useful books on various aspects of the subject. The most detailed and scholarly work providing complete factual information about Shakespeare is Sir Edmund Chambers, *William Shakespeare: A Study of Facts and Problems* (2 vols., Oxford, 1930). For detailed, factual information about the Elizabethan and seventeenth-century stages, the definitive reference works are Sir Edmund Chambers, *The Elizabethan Stage* (4 vols., Oxford, 1923) and Gerald E. Bentley, *The Jacobean and Caroline Stage* (5 vols., Oxford, 1941–1956). Alfred Harbage, *Shakespeare's Audience* (New York, 1941) throws light on the nature and tastes of the customers for whom Elizabethan dramatists wrote.

Although specialists disagree about details of stage construction, the reader will find essential information in John C. Adams, *The Globe Playhouse: Its Design and Equipment* (Barnes & Noble, 1961). A model of the Globe playhouse by Dr. Adams is on permanent exhibition in the Folger Shakespeare Library in Washington, D.C. An excellent description of the architecture of the Globe is Irwin Smith, *Shakespeare's Globe Playhouse: A Modern Reconstruction in Text and Scale Drawings Based upon the Reconstruction of the Globe by John Cranford Adams* (New York, 1956). Another recent study of the physical characteristics of the Globe is C. Walter Hodges, *The Globe Restored* (London, 1953). An easily read history of the early theatres is J. Q. Adams, *Shakespearean Playhouse: A History of English Theatres from the Beginnings to the Restoration* (Boston, 1917).

The question of the authenticity of Shakespeare's plays arouses perennial attention. A book that demolishes the notion of hidden cryptograms in the plays is William F. Friedman and Elizebeth S. Friedman, *The Shakespearean Ciphers Examined* (New York, 1957). A succinct account of the various absurdities advanced to suggest the authorship of a multitude of candidates other than Shakespeare will be found in R. C. Churchill, *Shakespeare and His Betters* (Bloomington, Ind., 1959) and Frank W. Wadsworth, *The Poacher from Stratford: A Partial Account of the Controversy over the Authorship of Shakespeare's Plays* (Berkeley, Calif., 1958). An essay on the curious notions in the writings of the anti-Shakespeareans is that by Louis B. Wright, "The Anti-Shakespeare Industry and the Growth of Cults," *The Virginia Quarterly Review*, XXXV (1959), 289-303.

The following titles on theatrical history will provide information about Shakespeare's plays in later periods: Alfred Harbage, *Theatre for Shakespeare* (Toronto, 1955); Esther Cloudman Dunn, *Shakespeare in America* (New York, 1939); George C. D. Odell, *Shakespeare from Betterton to Irving* (2 vols., London, 1921); Arthur Colby Sprague, *Shakespeare and the Actors: The Stage Business in His Plays (1660-1905)* (Cambridge, Mass., 1944) and *Shakespearian Players and Performances* (Cambridge, Mass., 1953); Leslie Hotson, *The Commonwealth and Restoration Stage* (Cambridge, Mass., 1928); Alwin Thaler, *Shakspere to Sheridan: A Book About the Theatre of Yesterday and To-day* (Cambridge, Mass., 1922); Ernest Bradlee Watson, *Sheridan to Robertson: A Study of the 19th-Century London Stage* (Cambridge, Mass., 1926). Enid Welsford, *The Court Masque* (Cambridge, Mass., 1927) is an excellent study of the characteristics of this form of entertainment.

Harley Granville-Barker, *Prefaces to Shakespeare* (5 vols., London, 1927-1948) provides stimulating critical discussion of the plays. An older classic of criticism is Andrew C. Bradley, *Shakespearean Tragedy: Lectures on Hamlet, Othello, King Lear, Macbeth* (London, 1904), which is now available in an inexpensive reprint (New York, 1955). Thomas M. Parrott, *Shakespearean Comedy* (New

York, 1949) is scholarly and readable. Shakespeare's dramatizations of English history are examined in E. M. W. Tillyard, *Shakespeare's History Plays* (London, 1948), and Lily Bess Campbell, *Shakespeare's "Histories," Mirrors of Elizabethan Policy* (San Marino, Calif., 1947) contains a more technical discussion of the same subject.

Reprints of some of the sources of Shakespeare's plays can be found in *Shakespeare's Library* (2 vols., 1850), edited by John Payne Collier, and *The Shakespeare Classics* (12 vols., 1907–1926), edited by Israel Gollancz. Geoffrey Bullough, *Narrative and Dramatic Sources of Shakespeare* (New York, 1957) is the first of a new series of volumes reprinting the sources. For discussion of Shakespeare's use of his sources see Kenneth Muir, *Shakespeare's Sources: Comedies and Tragedies* (London, 1957). Thomas M. Cranfill has recently edited a facsimile reprint of *Riche His Farewell to Military Profession* (1581), which contains stories that Shakespeare probably used for several of his plays.

For the historical background of *Henry V*, the reader may consult an exhaustive work by J. H. Wylie, *The Reign of Henry the Fifth* (3 vols., Cambridge, Eng., 1914–1929). A briefer book is E. F. Jacob, *Henry V and the Invasion of France* (New York, 1950). It is instructive to read Holinshed's version and compare it with Shakespeare's treatment. This can be done conveniently in *Holinshed's Chronicle as Used in Shakespeare's Plays,* edited by Allardyce Nicoll and Josephine Nicoll, (Everyman's Library; New York, 1951).

A discussion of the possible shorthand source for the First Quarto is that by H. T. Price, *The Text of Henry V* (Newcastle-under-Lyme, 1921), but this should be read in connection with the objections of other textual critics. Stimulating discussion of this and other critical problems will be found in the introductions by J. H. Walter to the new Arden edition (London, 1954) and by J. Dover Wilson to the new Cambridge edition (Cambridge, Eng., 1947).

Interesting pictures as well as new information about Shakespeare will be found in F. E. Halliday, *Shakespeare, a Pictorial Biography* (London, 1956). Allardyce Nicoll, *The Elizabethans* (Cambridge, Eng., 1957) contains a variety of illustrations.

A brief, clear, and accurate account of Tudor history is S. T. Bindoff, *The Tudors,* in the Penguin series. A readable general history is G. M. Trevelyan, *The History of England,* first published in 1926 and available in many editions. G. M. Trevelyan, *English Social History,* first published in 1942 and also available in many editions, provides fascinating information about England in all periods. Sir John Neale, *Queen Elizabeth* (London, 1934) is the best study of the great Queen. Various aspects of life in the Elizabethan period are treated in Louis B. Wright, *Middle-Class Culture in Elizabethan England* (Chapel Hill, N.C., 1935; reprinted by Cornell University Press, 1958). *Shakespeare's England: An Account of the Life and Manners of*

His Age, edited by Sidney Lee and C. T. Onions (2 vols., Oxford, 1916), provides a large amount of information on many aspects of life in the Elizabethan period. Additional information will be found in Muriel St. C. Byrne, *Elizabethan Life in Town and Country* (Barnes & Noble, 1961).

The Folger Shakespeare Library is currently publishing a series of illustrated pamphlets on various aspects of English life in the sixteenth and seventeenth centuries. The following titles are available: Dorothy E. Mason, *Music in Elizabethan England;* Craig R. Thompson, *The English Church in the Sixteenth Century;* Louis B. Wright, *Shakespeare's Theatre and the Dramatic Tradition;* Giles E. Dawson, *The Life of William Shakespeare;* Virginia A. LaMar, *English Dress in the Age of Shakespeare;* Craig R. Thompson, *The Bible in English, 1525-1611;* Craig R. Thompson, *Schools in Tudor England;* Craig R. Thompson, *Universities in Tudor England;* Lilly C. Stone, *English Sports and Recreations;* Conyers Read, *The Government of England under Elizabeth.*

Chorus.

King Henry the Fifth.
Duke of Gloucester,
Duke of Bedford, } brothers to the King.
Duke of Exeter, uncle to the *King.*
Duke of York, cousin to the *King.*
Earl of Salisbury.
Earl of Westmoreland.
Earl of Warwick.
Archbishop of Canterbury.
Bishop of Ely.
Earl of Cambridge.
Lord Scroop.
Sir Thomas Grey.
Sir Thomas Erpingham,
Gower, an English captain,
Fluellen, a Welsh captain, } officers in *King Henry's*
Macmorris, an Irish captain, army.
Jamy, a Scottish captain,
John Bates,
Alexander Court, } soldiers in the same.
Michael Williams,
Pistol.
Nym.
Bardolph.
Boy.
A Herald.

Charles the Sixth, King of France.
Lewis, the Dauphin.
Duke of Burgundy.
Duke of Orleans.
Duke of Bourbon.
Duke of Britaine.
The Constable of France.

Rambures, ⎫
Grandpré, ⎬ French lords.
Beaumont, ⎭
Governor of Harfleur.
Montjoy, a French herald.
Ambassadors to the *King of England.*

Isabel, Queen of France.
Katherine, daughter to the French King and Queen.
Alice, an attendant to *Katherine.*
Hostess Quickly, wife to *Pistol.*

Lords, Ladies, Officers, Soldiers, Citizens, Messengers, and Attendants.

SCENE:—*England and France.*]

THE LIFE OF
KING HENRY
THE FIFTH

ACT I

Pro. I. The player representing the Prologue apologizes for the efforts of the playwright and the actors to represent so great a theme, and urges the audience's indulgence and the co-operation of their imagination in witnessing the scenes to follow.

▪▪▪▪▪▪▪▪▪▪▪▪▪▪▪▪▪▪▪▪▪▪▪▪▪▪▪▪▪▪

1-2. a Muse of fire, that would ascend/ The brightest heaven of invention: an inspiration as vivid and powerful as fire, which would surpass the most lofty and brilliant invention.

4. swelling: magnificent, stirring.

5. like himself: in his own person.

6. port: appearance and bearing.

9. Crouch for employment: make ready for action; **gentles:** ladies and gentlemen; gentlefolk.

10. flat unraised: dull and earthbound.

11. scaffold: platform, stage.

12. cockpit: arena.

14. wooden O: an indication that the playhouse where *Henry V* was imagined as being performed was circular in shape; **the very casques:** even the helmets worn in the battle.

17. Attest: stand in place of.

18. ciphers to this great accompt: mere zeros in comparison with the great sum we represent. There is a play on **accompt** (account) meaning both a sum and a narrative.

19. imaginary forces: forces of imagination.

23. The perilous narrow ocean parts asunder: i.e., only the English Channel keeps the two haughty nations apart.

Enter *Prologue*.

O for a Muse of fire, that would ascend
The brightest heaven of invention,
A kingdom for a stage, princes to act,
And monarchs to behold the swelling scene!
Then should the warlike Harry, like himself,   5
Assume the port of Mars, and at his heels
(Leashed in, like hounds) should famine, sword,
      and fire
Crouch for employment. But pardon, gentles all,
The flat unraised spirits that hath dared   10
On this unworthy scaffold to bring forth
So great an object. Can this cockpit hold
The vasty fields of France? Or may we cram
Within this wooden O the very casques
That did affright the air at Agincourt?   15
O pardon, since a crooked figure may
Attest in little place a million,
And let us, ciphers to this great accompt,
On your imaginary forces work.
Suppose within the girdle of these walls   20
Are now confined two mighty monarchies,
Whose high-upreared and abutting fronts
The perilous narrow ocean parts asunder.
Piece out our imperfections with your thoughts:
Into a thousand parts divide one man   25

26. **puissance:** power, military might. Pronunciation here is trisyllabic.

28. **proud:** high-mettled, spirited.

31-2. **Turning the accomplishment of many years/ Into an hourglass:** telescoping the deeds done over many years in order to present them in a short space of time; **for the which supply:** for this function; i.e., to supply the information required.

━━━━━━━━━━━━━━━━━━━━━━━━━

I. i. The Archbishop of Canterbury and the Bishop of Ely are troubled at the threat to some of the church's revenues by the terms of a bill recently presented for consideration. The Archbishop, however, describes the reformation of King Henry since he ascended the throne and is encouraged by the King's show of dignity and religious devotion to believe that he may take the part of the church in the matter. As an added persuasion he has offered the King an unusually large sum of money to support a projected campaign in France. In a recent audience he had been about to inform the King of the facts pertaining to his claim to lands in France when they were interrupted by the arrival of a French Ambassador. It being now the time for the Ambassador's audience, they depart for the presence chamber.

━━━━━━━━━━━━━━━━━━━━━━━━━

1. **self:** selfsame; **urged:** presented for consideration, not urged in the modern sense.

3. **Was like:** that is, came close to passing.

4. **scambling:** scrambling, disorderly.

9. **temporal:** used for secular purposes; probably lands from which the church derived an income, such as farming lands, etc.

And make imaginary puissance.
Think, when we talk of horses, that you see them
Printing their proud hoofs i' the receiving earth.
For 'tis your thoughts that now must deck our kings,
Carry them here and there, jumping o'er times,   30
Turning the accomplishment of many years
Into an hourglass; for the which supply,
Admit me Chorus to this history,
Who, Prologue-like, your humble patience pray,
Gently to hear, kindly to judge our play.   35

Exit.

ACT I

Scene I. [London. An antechamber in the King's
Palace.]

Enter the two *Bishops*—[the *Archbishop*] *of
Canterbury* and [the *Bishop of*] *Ely*.

Cant. My lord, I'll tell you, that self bill is urged
Which in the eleventh year of the last king's reign
Was like, and had indeed against us passed
But that the scambling and unquiet time
Did push it out of farther question.   5
  Ely. But how, my lord, shall we resist it now?
  Cant. It must be thought on. If it pass against us,
We lose the better half of our possession;
For all the temporal lands which men devout
By testament have given to the Church   10

15. **lazars:** lepers, literally, though persons with any incurable and loathsome disease were so described.

16. **corporal:** bodily.

22. **what prevention:** what can we do to prevent this.

23. **full of grace and fair regard:** very gracious and benevolent in attitude.

27. **mortified:** deadened, killed.

29. **Consideration:** reflection in a special theological sense; a thorough examination of the state of his soul.

30. **the offending Adam:** human sinfulness.

35. **currance:** current, flux; possibly from the contemporary French *courrance*.

36. **Hydra-headed:** i.e., many-headed and difficult to overcome, like the mythological Hydra, a creature with nine heads, which grew two more for every one cut off.

37. **his:** its.

40. **divinity:** theology.

Would they strip from us; being valued thus—
As much as would maintain, to the King's honor,
Full fifteen earls and fifteen hundred knights,
Six thousand and two hundred good esquires,
And, to relief of lazars and weak age,   15
Of indigent faint souls, past corporal toil,
A hundred almshouses right well supplied;
And to the coffers of the King beside,
A thousand pounds by the year. Thus runs the bill.
    Ely. This would drink deep.   20
    Cant.   'Twould drink the cup and all.
    Ely. But what prevention?
    Cant. The King is full of grace and fair regard.
    Ely. And a true lover of the holy Church.
    Cant. The courses of his youth promised it not.   25
The breath no sooner left his father's body
But that his wildness, mortified in him,
Seemed to die too. Yea, at that very moment
Consideration like an angel came
And whipped the offending Adam out of him,   30
Leaving his body as a paradise
T' envelop and contain celestial spirits.
Never was such a sudden scholar made;
Never came reformation in a flood
With such a heady currance scouring faults;   35
Nor never Hydra-headed willfulness
So soon did lose his seat, and all at once,
As in this king.
    Ely.   We are blessed in the change.
    Cant. Hear him but reason in divinity,   40
And, all-admiring, with an inward wish

47. **policy:** statecraft.

48. **Gordian knot:** apparently insoluble difficulty. Gordius, an ancient king of Phrygia, tied a knot in a piece of bark to hold together the pole and yoke of his chariot; an oracle decreed that whoever could untie the knot would rule all Asia. Alexander the Great, failing to untie it, cut the knot with his sword and claimed to have fulfilled the prophecy.

49. **Familiar as his garter:** with as much ease as he might unfasten his own garter.

50. **chartered libertine:** one licensed to go anywhere at will.

51. **the mute wonder lurketh in men's ears:** i.e., wonder keeps men silent and forces them to listen. The charm of the King's utterance is such that it excites envious admiration.

53-4. **the art and practic part of life/ Must be the mistress to this theoric:** training and practical experience would appear to be responsible for the ideas he expresses.

56. **vain:** profitless.

60. **sequestration:** withdrawal.

61. **open haunts and popularity:** public places and the common throng.

68. **crescive in his faculty:** growing in its potentiality. **His,** as above in l. 37, is often used for the neuter genitive.

70. **we must needs admit the means:** there is no alternative to accepting a natural explanation.

You would desire the King were made a prelate;
Hear him debate of commonwealth affairs,
You would say it hath been all in all his study;
List his discourse of war, and you shall hear   45
A fearful battle rend'red you in music;
Turn him to any cause of policy,
The Gordian knot of it he will unloose,
Familiar as his garter; that, when he speaks,
The air, a chartered libertine, is still,   50
And the mute wonder lurketh in men's ears
To steal his sweet and honeyed sentences;
So that the art and practic part of life
Must be the mistress to this theoric;
Which is a wonder how his Grace should glean it,   55
Since his addiction was to courses vain,
His companies unlettered, rude, and shallow,
His hours filled up with riots, banquets, sports;
And never noted in him any study,
Any retirement, any sequestration   60
From open haunts and popularity.

Ely. The strawberry grows underneath the nettle,
And wholesome berries thrive and ripen best
Neighbored by fruit of baser quality;
And so the Prince obscured his contemplation   65
Under the veil of wildness, which (no doubt)
Grew like the summer grass, fastest by night,
Unseen, yet crescive in his faculty.

Cant. It must be so; for miracles are ceased,
And therefore we must needs admit the means   70
How things are perfected.

Ely.   But, my good lord,

74. **Urged:** presented; see l. 1.

76. **indifferent:** impartial.

78. **exhibiters:** introducers; those supporting the bill.

80. **Upon:** as a result of; **our spiritual Convocation:** an assembly of the religious officials of the kingdom.

82. **opened:** revealed; **at large:** in full.

89. **would fain have:** would like to have.

90. **severals:** various points; **unhidden passages:** obvious descent.

93. **Edward:** Edward III, whose mother, Isabella, was daughter of the French king Philip IV.

102. **wait upon you:** accompany you.

Hercules slaying the Hydra.
From Lodovico Dolce, *Le trasformationi* (1570).
(See I. i. 36.)

5

How now for mitigation of this bill
Urged by the commons? Doth his Majesty
Incline to it, or no?   75
 Cant.   He seems indifferent;
Or rather swaying more upon our part
Than cherishing the exhibiters against us;
For I have made an offer to his Majesty—
Upon our spiritual Convocation,   80
And in regard of causes now in hand,
Which I have opened to his Grace at large,
As touching France—to give a greater sum
Than ever at one time the clergy yet
Did to his predecessors part withal.   85
 Ely. How did this offer seem received, my lord?
 Cant. With good acceptance of his Majesty;
Save that there was not time enough to hear,
As I perceived his Grace would fain have done,
The severals and unhidden passages   90
Of his true titles to some certain dukedoms,
And generally to the crown and seat of France,
Derived from Edward, his great-grandfather.
 Ely. What was the impediment that broke this off?
 Cant. The French ambassador upon that instant   95
Craved audience; and the hour I think is come
To give him hearing. Is it four o'clock?
 Ely. It is.
 Cant. Then go we in to know his embassy,
Which I could with a ready guess declare   100
Before the Frenchman speak a word of it.
 Ely. I'll wait upon you, and I long to hear it.
            Exeunt.

I. [ii.] The Archbishop of Canterbury informs the King that the French denial of his claim to lands in France is unjustifiably based on the supposed "Salic law." He urges the King to fight for his claim, invoking the names of his great-grandfather, Edward III, and Edward, the Black Prince, and offering a large sum from church funds to support the campaign. The King states his determination to fight for his rights in France.

Ambassadors from France are then admitted. The spokesman brings a reply from the Dauphin to Henry heaping contempt upon Henry for his well-known riotous living as prince, and a gift of tennis balls as a symbol of the sort of activity for which he is best suited. Henry's resolve is strengthened by this insult, and he returns a threat to make the Dauphin and all France regret the frivolous reaction to his claim.

▬▬▬▬▬▬▬▬▬▬

5. resolved: determined, satisfied.

7. task our thoughts: trouble my mind. Henry uses the royal plural.

13. the Law Salique: originally the body of laws of the Salian Franks, later a term applied to the principle that the female could not inherit the French throne.

14. Or: either.

16. fashion, wrest, or bow your reading: the three words are synonymous: distort your interpretation.

17-9. nicely charge . . . truth: lay a burden of guilt upon your soul by your sophistry in describing as rightful claims which you know to be illegal.

[Scene II. London. The presence chamber in the
Palace.]

Enter the *King, Humphrey* [*Duke of Gloucester*],
Bedford, Clarence, Warwick, Westmoreland, and
Exeter, [with *Attendants*].

King. Where is my gracious Lord of Canterbury?
Exe. Not here in presence.
King.   Send for him, good uncle.
West. Shall we call in the ambassador, my liege?
King. Not yet, my cousin. We would be resolved,   5
Before we hear him, of some things of weight,
That task our thoughts, concerning us and France.

Enter two *Bishops* [—the *Archbishop of Canterbury*
and the *Bishop of Ely*].

Cant. God and his angels guard your sacred throne
And make you long become it!
King.   Sure we thank you.   10
My learned lord, we pray you to proceed
And justly and religiously unfold
Why the Law Salique, that they have in France,
Or should or should not bar us in our claim.
And God forbid, my dear and faithful lord,   15
That you should fashion, wrest, or bow your reading,
Or nicely charge your understanding soul
With opening titles miscreate whose right
Suits not in native colors with the truth;
For God doth know how many, now in health,   20

21. **approbation:** support.

23. **impawn:** pledge; i.e., invoke our royal pledge to go to war.

29-30. **... wrongs gives edge unto the swords/ That makes such waste in brief mortality:** Elizabethans were less particular than moderns about the agreement of subject and predicate.

38. **imperial:** the Archbishop includes France as part of the English King's dominions.

40. **Pharamond:** a legendary king of the Salian Franks.

43. **gloze:** interpret.

King Pharamond.
From H. C., *Abbrege de l'histoire françoise* (1596).

7

Shall drop their blood in approbation
Of what your reverence shall incite us to.
Therefore take heed how you impawn our person,
How you awake our sleeping sword of war.
We charge you in the name of God, take heed;   25
For never two such kingdoms did contend
Without much fall of blood, whose guiltless drops
Are every one a woe, a sore complaint
'Gainst him whose wrongs gives edge unto the swords
That makes such waste in brief mortality.   30
Under this conjuration speak, my lord;
For we will hear, note, and believe in heart
That what you speak is in your conscience washed
As pure as sin with baptism.
     Cant. Then hear me, gracious sovereign, and you   35
       peers,
That owe yourselves, your lives, and services
To this imperial throne. There is no bar
To make against your Highness' claim to France
But this which they produce from Pharamond: 40
"In terram Salicam mulieres ne succedant";
"No woman shall succeed in Salique land."
Which Salique land the French unjustly gloze
To be the realm of France, and Pharamond
The founder of this law and female bar.   45
Yet their own authors faithfully affirm
That the land Salique is in Germany,
Between the floods of Sala and of Elbe;
Where Charles the Great, having subdued the Saxons,
There left behind and settled certain French;   50
Who, holding in disdain the German women

King Pepin.
From H. C., *Abbrege de l'histoire françoise* (1598).

52. **dishonest:** unchaste.

61. **defunction:** death.

62. **Idly:** foolishly.

69. **heir general:** heir-at-law, including female heirs; in other words, the lawful heir whether of male or female descent.

75. **find:** supply.

77. **Conveyed himself:** passed himself off; **Lingare:** Lingard in Holinshed.

78. **Charlemain:** historically, Charles the Bald. Shakespeare took the error from his source, either Holinshed or Hall.

80. **Lewis the Tenth:** actually, Louis IX; an error from Holinshed.

For some dishonest manners of their life,
Established then this law: to wit, no female
Should be inheritrix in Salique land;
Which Salique (as I said) 'twixt Elbe and Sala   55
Is at this day in Germany called Meisen.
Then doth it well appear the Salique Law
Was not devised for the realm of France;
Nor did the French possess the Salique land
Until four hundred one and twenty years   60
After defunction of King Pharamond,
Idly supposed the founder of this law,
Who died within the year of our redemption
Four hundred twenty-six; and Charles the Great
Subdued the Saxons, and did seat the French   65
Beyond the river Sala, in the year
Eight hundred five. Besides, their writers say,
King Pepin, which deposed Childeric,
Did, as heir general, being descended
Of Blithild, which was daughter to King Clothair,   70
Make claim and title to the crown of France.
Hugh Capet also—who usurped the crown
Of Charles the Duke of Lorraine, sole heir male
Of the true line and stock of Charles the Great—
To find his title with some shows of truth,   75
Though in pure truth it was corrupt and naught,
Conveyed himself as the heir to the Lady Lingare,
Daughter of Charlemain, who was the son
To Lewis the Emperor, and Lewis the son
Of Charles the Great. Also King Lewis the Tenth,   80
Who was sole heir to the usurper Capet,
Could not keep quiet in his conscience,

85. **Ermengare:** Ermengard in Holinshed.

91. **Lewis his satisfaction:** i.e., Lewis' satisfaction.

96. **hide them in a net:** proverbial: conceal themselves in an intricate but transparent device.

97. **imbare:** expose.

111. **defeat:** i.e., the Battle of Crécy in 1346.

Hugh Capet.
From H. C., *Abbrege de l'histoire françoise* (1596).

Wearing the crown of France, till satisfied
That fair Queen Isabel, his grandmother,
Was lineal of the Lady Ermengare, 85
Daughter to Charles the foresaid Duke of Lorraine;
By the which marriage the line of Charles the Great
Was reunited to the crown of France.
So that, as clear as is the summer's sun,
King Pepin's title and Hugh Capet's claim, 90
King Lewis his satisfaction, all appear
To hold in right and title of the female.
So do the kings of France unto this day,
Howbeit they would hold up this Salique Law
To bar your Highness claiming from the female, 95
And rather choose to hide them in a net
Than amply to imbare their crooked titles
Usurped from you and your progenitors.
   King. May I with right and conscience make this
      claim? 100
   Cant. The sin upon my head, dread sovereign!
For in the Book of Numbers is it writ:
When the man dies, let the inheritance
Descend unto the daughter. Gracious lord,
Stand for your own, unwind your bloody flag, 105
Look back into your mighty ancestors;
Go, my dread lord, to your great-grandsire's tomb,
From whom you claim; invoke his warlike spirit,
And your great-uncle's, Edward the Black Prince,
Who on the French ground played a tragedy, 110
Making defeat on the full power of France,
Whiles his most mighty father on a hill
Stood smiling to behold his lion's whelp

115. **entertain:** engage, take on.

118. **action:** i.e., lack of action.

123. **thrice-puissant:** that is, puissant yourself and triply so for having two such valiant ancestors.

134. **pavilioned in the fields of France:** as though camping out before the battle.

137. **spiritualty:** church.

142. **lay down our proportions:** allocate the necessary troops.

143. **road:** inroad.

144. **With all advantages:** with everything favorable to their success.

Charlemagne.
From H. C., *Abbrege de l'histoire françoise* (1596).
(See I. ii. 78.)

10

Forage in blood of French nobility.
O noble English, that could entertain   115
With half their forces the full pride of France
And let another half stand laughing by,
All out of work and cold for action!

　Ely. Awake remembrance of these valiant dead
And with your puissant arm renew their feats.   120
You are their heir; you sit upon their throne;
The blood and courage that renowned them
Runs in your veins; and my thrice-puissant liege
Is in the very May-morn of his youth,
Ripe for exploits and mighty enterprises.   125

　Exe. Your brother kings and monarchs of the earth
Do all expect that you should rouse yourself,
As did the former lions of your blood.

　West. They know your Grace hath cause and
　　means and might;   130
So hath your Highness. Never king of England
Had nobles richer and more loyal subjects,
Whose hearts have left their bodies here in England
And lie pavilioned in the fields of France.

　Cant. O let their bodies follow, my dear liege,   135
With blood and sword and fire, to win your right!
In aid whereof we of the spiritualty
Will raise your Highness such a mighty sum
As never did the clergy at one time
Bring in to any of your ancestors.   140

　King. We must not only arm t' invade the French,
But lay down our proportions to defend
Against the Scot, who will make road upon us
With all advantages.

145. **marches:** borders.

148. **coursing snatchers:** raiders who gain small prizes by speedy surprise attacks. The contrast is with the action of troops in an organized military effort.

149. **main intendment:** i.e., what the nation as a whole may do.

150. **giddy:** unreliable.

153. **unfurnished:** unprotected.

156. **Galling:** harassing; **gleaned:** stripped; left undefended.

160. **feared:** frightened.

167. **The King of Scots:** David II, captured by the English in 1346 while Edward III was fighting in France.

170. **ooze and bottom:** oozy bottom.

171. **wrack:** wreck; **sumless:** priceless, invaluable.

Cant. They of those marches, gracious sovereign, 145
Shall be a wall sufficient to defend
Our inland from the pilfering borderers.

King. We do not mean the coursing snatchers only,
But fear the main intendment of the Scot,
Who hath been still a giddy neighbor to us;   150
For you shall read that my great-grandfather
Never went with his forces into France
But that the Scot on his unfurnished kingdom
Came pouring like the tide into a breach,
With ample and brim fullness of his force,   155
Galling the gleaned land with hot assays,
Girding with grievous siege castles and towns;
That England, being empty of defense,
Hath shook and trembled at the ill neighborhood.

Cant. She hath been then more feared than 160
    harmed, my liege;
For hear her but exampled by herself:
When all her chivalry hath been in France,
And she a mourning widow of her nobles,
She hath herself not only well defended   165
But taken and impounded as a stray
The King of Scots; whom she did send to France
To fill King Edward's fame with prisoner kings,
And make her chronicle as rich with praise
As is the ooze and bottom of the sea   170
With sunken wrack and sumless treasuries.

Ely. But there's a saying very old and true—

      "If that you will France win,
        Then with Scotland first begin."

179. **tame:** attame; break into so as to spoil; **havoc:** damage.

181. **crushed necessity:** that is, crushed so as to be powerless by the measures he suggests to combat the Scots.

184. **While that:** while.

185. **advised:** circumspect, prudent.

187. **keep in one consent:** stay in harmony.

188. **Congreeing:** agreeing with each other; **close:** a play on two meanings: cadence, the musical term; and union.

193. **butt:** archery target.

195. **a rule in nature:** the pattern of behavior which is natural to them.

196. **The act of order:** the method by which order should be established and maintained.

201. **Make boot upon:** plunder, despoil.

204. **busied in his majesty:** kept busy by his royal responsibilities.

For once the eagle (England) being in prey,   175
To her unguarded nest the weasel (Scot)
Comes sneaking, and so sucks her princely eggs,
Playing the mouse in absence of the cat,
To tame and havoc more than she can eat.

   Exe. It follows then, the cat must stay at home.   180
Yet that is but a crushed necessity,
Since we have locks to safeguard necessaries,
And pretty traps to catch the petty thieves.
While that the armed hand doth fight abroad,
The advised head defends itself at home;   185
For government, though high, and low, and lower,
Put into parts, doth keep in one consent,
Congreeing in a full and natural close,
Like music.

   Cant.   Therefore doth heaven divide   190
The state of man in divers functions,
Setting endeavor in continual motion;
To which is fixed as an aim or butt
Obedience; for so work the honeybees,
Creatures that by a rule in nature teach   195
The act of order to a peopled kingdom.
They have a king, and officers of sorts,
Where some like magistrates correct at home,
Others like merchants venture trade abroad,
Others like soldiers armed in their stings   200
Make boot upon the summer's velvet buds,
Which pillage they with merry march bring home
To the tent-royal of their emperor,
Who, busied in his majesty, surveys
The singing masons building roofs of gold,   205

206. **civil:** orderly in behavior.

207. **mechanic:** usually applied to the unskilled laboring class in contempt or condescending sympathy.

209. **sad-eyed:** grave in expression.

212-13. **having full reference/ To one consent:** all entirely relating to the same end.

217. **dial:** sundial.

227. **name of:** reputation for; **hardiness and policy:** valor and shrewdness.

229. **Dauphin:** heir-apparent to the throne of France.

232. **our awe:** i.e., awe of us.

234. **empery:** sovereignty.

The civil citizens kneading up the honey,
The poor mechanic porters crowding in
Their heavy burdens at his narrow gate,
The sad-eyed justice, with his surly hum,
Delivering o'er to executors pale   210
The lazy yawning drone. I this infer,
That many things having full reference
To one consent may work contrariously,
As many arrows loosed several ways
Come to one mark, as many ways meet in one town, 215
As many fresh streams meet in one salt sea,
As many lines close in the dial's center;
So may a thousand actions, once afoot,
End in one purpose, and be all well borne
Without defeat. Therefore to France, my liege!   220
Divide your happy England into four;
Whereof take you one quarter into France,
And you withal shall make all Gallia shake.
If we, with thrice such powers left at home,
Cannot defend our own doors from the dog,   225
Let us be worried, and our nation lose
The name of hardiness and policy.
    King. Call in the messengers sent from the
        Dauphin.
                        [*Exeunt some Attendants.*]
Now are we well resolved, and by God's help   230
And yours, the noble sinews of our power,
France being ours, we'll bend it to our awe,
Or break it all to pieces. Or there we'll sit,
Ruling in large and ample empery
O'er France and all her (almost) kingly dukedoms, 235

241. **worshiped:** honored; **waxen epitaph:** that is, lacking even a perishable obituary, let alone one carved in brass or stone as was usual on funeral monuments.

247. **what we have in charge:** i.e., the message entrusted to me.

248. **sparingly show you far off:** that is, beat around the bush discreetly.

251. **grace:** probably a combination of "gracious inclination" and "Christian virtue." See "The King is full of grace and fair regard" at I. i. 24.

255. **few:** few words.

260. **savor:** smack, taste.

261. **advised:** cautious, thoughtful; see l. 185.

262. **galliard:** sprightly dance.

Or lay these bones in an unworthy urn,
Tombless, with no remembrance over them.
Either our history shall with full mouth
Speak freely of our acts, or else our grave,
Like Turkish mute, shall have a tongueless mouth,   240
Not worshiped with a waxen epitaph.

Enter Ambassadors of France, [attended].

Now are we well prepared to know the pleasure
Of our fair cousin Dauphin; for we hear
Your greeting is from him, not from the King.
   Ambassador. May't please your Majesty to give us   245
      leave
Freely to render what we have in charge;
Or shall we sparingly show you far off
The Dauphin's meaning, and our embassy?
   King. We are no tyrant, but a Christian king,   250
Unto whose grace our passion is as subject
As is our wretches fett'red in our prisons.
Therefore with frank and with uncurbed plainness
Tell us the Dauphin's mind.
   Ambassador.   Thus then, in few: 255
Your Highness, lately sending into France,
Did claim some certain dukedoms, in the right
Of your great predecessor, King Edward the Third.
In answer of which claim, the Prince our master
Says that you savor too much of your youth,   260
And bids you be advised. There's naught in France
That can be with a nimble galliard won;
You cannot revel into dukedoms there.

264. **meeter:** more suitable.

265. **tun:** barrel.

275. **crown:** both the obvious literal meaning and the name for a stake when betting on a tennis match; **hazard:** another play on words. A **hazard** was a part of the tennis court, and a point was scored when the ball was hit into it.

278. **chases:** military forays; also a technical tennis term for another way to score a point.

279. **comes o'er us:** puts us down.

285. **state:** regal pomp and dignity.

286. **show my sail of greatness:** display the full power of my rank and station.

287. **rouse me:** raise myself up; elevate myself.

288-89. **For that I have laid by my majesty/ And plodded like a man for working days:** in order to be able to seat myself on the French throne I have lived like a common member of the working class. This excuse rings a little falsely in the ear and does not overcome the difficulty many critics have seen in the change between Henry V and the Prince Hal of Shakespeare's *Henry IV*.

294. **gunstones:** cannonballs, which were actually made of stone.

He therefore sends you, meeter for your spirit,
This tun of treasure; and, in lieu of this, 265
Desires you let the dukedoms that you claim
Hear no more of you. This the Dauphin speaks.
  King. What treasure, uncle?
  Exe.   Tennis balls, my liege.
  King. We are glad the Dauphin is so pleasant 270
    with us.
His present and your pains we thank you for.
When we have matched our rackets to these balls,
We will in France (by God's grace) play a set
Shall strike his father's crown into the hazard. 275
Tell him he hath made a match with such a wrangler
That all the courts of France will be disturbed
With chases. And we understand him well,
How he comes o'er us with our wilder days,
Not measuring what use we made of them. 280
We never valued this poor seat of England,
And therefore, living hence, did give ourself
To barbarous license; as 'tis ever common
That men are merriest when they are from home.
But tell the Dauphin I will keep my state, 285
Be like a king, and show my sail of greatness,
When I do rouse me in my throne of France.
For that I have laid by my majesty
And plodded like a man for working days.
But I will rise there with so full a glory 290
That I will dazzle all the eyes of France,
Yea, strike the Dauphin blind to look on us.
And tell the pleasant Prince this mock of his
Hath turned his balls to gunstones, and his soul

295. **Shall stand sore charged:** will be severely blamed.

313. **omit:** overlook; **happy:** favorable.

316. **those to God, that run before our business:** i.e., the proper religious devotion that should be observed before such an undertaking.

320. **God before:** God leading us.

322. **task:** tax, strain to the utmost; see l. 7.

Swift Mercury.
From Innocenzio Ringhieri, *Cento giuochi liberali* (1551).
(See Cho. [II.] 7.)

16

Shall stand sore charged for the wasteful vengeance 295
That shall fly with them; for many a thousand
     widows
Shall this his mock mock out of their dear husbands,
Mock mothers from their sons, mock castles down;
And some are yet ungotten and unborn   300
That shall have cause to curse the Dauphin's scorn.
But this lies all within the will of God,
To whom I do appeal, and in whose name,
Tell you the Dauphin, I am coming on,
To venge me as I may and to put forth   305
My rightful hand in a well-hallowed cause.
So get you hence in peace. And tell the Dauphin
His jest will savor but of shallow wit
When thousands weep more than did laugh at it.
Convey them with safe conduct. Fare you well.   310
                         Exeunt Ambassadors.
     Exe. This was a merry message.
     King. We hope to make the sender blush at it.
Therefore, my lords, omit no happy hour
That may give furth'rance to our expedition;
For we have now no thought in us but France,   315
Save those to God, that run before our business.
Therefore let our proportions for these wars
Be soon collected, and all things thought upon
That may with reasonable swiftness add
More feathers to our wings; for, God before,   320
We'll chide this Dauphin at his father's door.
Therefore let every man now task his thought
That this fair action may on foot be brought.
                              Exeunt.

THE LIFE OF
KING HENRY
THE FIFTH

ACT II

Cho. [II.] The Chorus describes the enthusiasm in England for Henry's campaign in France but warns of the treason of Richard, Earl of Cambridge; Henry, Lord Scroop of Masham; and Sir Thomas Grey.

—————————————————————————

Ent. Flourish: the sounding of a trumpet.

2. **silken dalliance:** both frivolity and the elegant attire worn for gaiety.

3. **honor's thought:** the thought of honor.

7. **English Mercuries:** the Englishmen, eager to follow the King to France, are described as rivaling Mercury, the messenger of the gods, in speed.

9. **hilts:** the two parts of the hilt, divided by the sword blade, were each considered a hilt.

10. **crowns imperial, crowns, and coronets:** crowns for emperors, kings, and nobility.

12. **intelligence:** espionage.

14. **pale policy:** weak and fearful statecraft.

18. **honor would thee do:** i.e., would be honorable for you to do; that honor demands.

19. **kind and natural:** filial according to nature's law; naturally filled with filial devotion.

21. **hollow:** empty; i.e., heartless; **bosoms:** both seats of affection and the bosoms of clothing, where money and letters were carried.

[*ACT II*]

Flourish. Enter *Chorus.*

Now all the youth of England are on fire,
And silken dalliance in the wardrobe lies.
Now thrive the armorers, and honor's thought
Reigns solely in the breast of every man.
They sell the pasture now to buy the horse,   5
Following the mirror of all Christian kings
With winged heels, as English Mercuries.
For now sits Expectation in the air
And hides a sword, from hilts unto the point,
With crowns imperial, crowns, and coronets   10
Promised to Harry and his followers.
The French, advised by good intelligence
Of this most dreadful preparation,
Shake in their fear and with pale policy
Seek to divert the English purposes.   15
O England! model to thy inward greatness,
Like little body with a mighty heart,
What mightst thou do that honor would thee do,
Were all thy children kind and natural!
But see, thy fault France hath in thee found out,   20
A nest of hollow bosoms, which he fills

22. **treacherous crowns:** French money for their treason.

26. **gilt . . . guilt:** a commonplace Elizabethan play on the two words.

28. **grace of kings:** model of a gracious king.

31-2. **we'll digest/ The abuse of distance, force a play:** we'll make as brief as possible the distances we must travel across time and space, and re-create events as well as we can on the stage.

40. **not offend one stomach:** not make anyone seasick, nor offend any critical taste.

42. **Southampton:** The Chorus is saying in this passage that when the King next appears we must imagine him at Southampton ready to sail for France.

━━━━━━━━━━━━━━━━━━━━━━━━━━

[II. i.] Bardolph and Pistol, companions of the King's wild youth, are introduced with Corporal Nym, a rival of Pistol for Hostess Quickly's affections. Nym is disposed to quarrel with Pistol, who has married the Hostess, though she was troth-plight to himself. Bardolph is trying to keep the peace when a boy reports that Falstaff is seriously ill and summons the Hostess to his side. Pistol and Nym are finally reconciled and the three men agree to go to France with the army to pick up what they can in the way of a dishonest living. The Hostess returns to take them to Falstaff, ill of a fever and heart-broken because of his desertion by the King.

━━━━━━━━━━━━━━━━━━━━━━━━━━

3. **Ancient:** a corruption of "ensign" or standard-bearer.

18

With treacherous crowns; and three corrupted men—
One, Richard Earl of Cambridge, and the second,
Henry Lord Scroop of Masham, and the third,
Sir Thomas Grey, knight, of Northumberland—   25
Have, for the gilt of France (O guilt indeed!)
Confirmed conspiracy with fearful France,
And by their hands this grace of kings must die,
If hell and treason hold their promises,
Ere he take ship for France, and in Southampton.   30
Linger your patience on and we'll digest
The abuse of distance, force a play.
The sum is paid, the traitors are agreed,
The King is set from London, and the scene
Is now transported, gentles, to Southampton.   35
There is the playhouse now, there must you sit,
And thence to France shall we convey you safe
And bring you back, charming the narrow seas
To give you gentle pass; for, if we may,
We'll not offend one stomach with our play.   40
But, till the King come forth, and not till then,
Unto Southampton do we shift our scene.

Exit.

[Scene I. London. A street.]

Enter *Corporal Nym* and *Lieutenant Bardolph.*

Bard. Well met, Corporal Nym.
Nym. Good morrow, Lieutenant Bardolph.
Bard. What, are Ancient Pistol and you friends yet?

4-5. when time shall serve: when a favorable opportunity occurs.

7. iron: sword.

11. sworn brothers: pledged to support each other in a career of thievery.

15-6. rest: firm resolve. In the card game called primero a player might "set up his rest" on the cards in his hand as a modern player might "stand pat"; **that is the rendezvous of it:** that's the sum of it all; that's all there is to it.

19. troth-plight: formally betrothed. In Elizabethan common-law usage, such a contract was almost as binding as marriage, though a church wedding was normally performed in due course.

23-4. Though patience be a tired mare, yet she will plod: i.e., my patience is failing but it has not yet given out.

29. tyke: mongrel dog.

Nym. For my part, I care not. I say little; but when
time shall serve, there shall be smiles—but that shall   5
be as it may. I dare not fight; but I will wink and
hold out mine iron. It is a simple one; but what
though? It will toast cheese, and it will endure cold
as another man's sword will—and there's an end.

Bard. I will bestow a breakfast to make you   10
friends, and we'll be all three sworn brothers to
France. Let't be so, good Corporal Nym.

Nym. Faith, I will live so long as I may, that's the
certain of it; and when I cannot live any longer, I
will do as I may. That is my rest, that is the rendez-   15
vous of it.

Bard. It is certain, Corporal, that he is married to
Nell Quickly, and certainly she did you wrong, for
you were troth-plight to her.

Nym. I cannot tell. Things must be as they may.   20
Men may sleep, and they may have their throats
about them at that time, and some say knives have
edges. It must be as it may. Though patience be a
tired mare, yet she will plod. There must be conclusions. Well, I cannot tell.   25

Enter *Pistol* and *Hostess Quickly.*

Bard. Here comes Ancient Pistol and his wife.
Good Corporal, be patient here. How now, mine host
Pistol?

Pist. Base tyke, callst thou me host?
Now by this hand I swear I scorn the term;   30
Nor shall my Nell keep lodgers!

36. here: the editor Charles Knight's suggestion to correct the Folio reading "hewne." The Quarto reads "O Lord heeres Corporall Nims."

41. Iceland dog: a long-haired lap dog.

45. shog off: come along; **solus:** alone. Pistol does not understand and considers it an insult.

46. egregious: extraordinary.

47. mervailous: spelled thus to indicate Pistol's accent, on the second syllable.

49. maw: stomach; **perdy:** by God, a corruption of French *par dieu*.

52. take: i.e., take fire; possibly with the second meaning "take offense."

54-9. Barbason: a demon; **I have an humor . . . that's the humor of it:** Nym's conversation in general satirizes contemporary fads of speech.

60. wight: fellow.

Host. No, by my troth, not long; for we cannot
lodge and board a dozen or fourteen gentlewomen
that live honestly by the prick of their needles but it
will be thought we keep a bawdy house straight. O   35
well-a-day, Lady, if he be not here now! We shall see
willful adultery and murder committed.

[*Nym and Pistol draw.*]

Bard. Good Lieutenant—good Corporal—offer nothing here.

Nym. Pish!   40

Pist. Pish for thee, Iceland dog! thou prick-eared
    cur of Iceland!

Host. Good Corporal Nym, show thy valor, and
put up your sword.

Nym. Will you shog off? I would have you solus.   45

Pist. "Solus," egregious dog? O viper vile!
The "solus" in thy most mervailous face!
The "solus" in thy teeth, and in thy throat,
And in thy hateful lungs, yea, in thy maw, perdy!
And, which is worse, within thy nasty mouth!   50
I do retort the "solus" in thy bowels;
For I can take, and Pistol's cock is up,
And flashing fire will follow.

Nym. I am not Barbason; you cannot conjure me. I
have an humor to knock you indifferently well. If you   55
grow foul with me, Pistol, I will scour you with my
rapier, as I may, in fair terms. If you would walk off,
I would prick your guts a little in good terms, as I
may, and that's the humor of it.

Pist. O braggart vile, and damned furious wight,   60

66. **mickle:** powerful, great.

68. **tall:** valiant.

71. **Couple a gorge:** Pistol's version of *couper la gorge,* the French for "cut the throat."

74. **spital:** hospital.

75. **powd'ring tub:** a treatment for venereal disease.

76. **lazar kite:** diseased whore; see **lazar,** I. i. 15; **Cressid;** Cressida, the beloved of Troilus in the legend used by Chaucer, Shakespeare, and others. In Robert Henryson's *Testament of Cresseid,* she died in leprous poverty.

78. **quondam:** erstwhile. Quickly, in other words, was her maiden name before she married Pistol.

79. **pauca:** in few words.

80. **Go to:** be off with you; that's enough of the subject.

86. **yield the crow a pudding:** i.e., become carrion flesh; die; a proverbial phrase.

The grave doth gape, and doting death is near.
Therefore exhale!

Bard. Hear me, hear me what I say! He that strikes
the first stroke, I'll run him up to the hilts, as I am a
soldier.   [*Draws.*]   65

Pist. An oath of mickle might, and fury shall abate.
                [*Pistol and Nym sheathe their swords.*]
Give me thy fist, thy forefoot to me give.
Thy spirits are most tall.

Nym. I will cut thy throat one time or other in fair
terms. That is the humor of it.   70

Pist. Couple a gorge!
That is the word. I thee defy again.
O hound of Crete, thinkst thou my spouse to get?
No; to the spital go,
And from the powd'ring tub of infamy   75
Fetch forth the lazar kite of Cressid's kind,
Doll Tearsheet, she by name, and her espouse.
I have, and I will hold, the quondam Quickly
For the only she; and—pauca, there's enough.
Go to!   80

Enter the *Boy*.

Boy. Mine host Pistol, you must come to my master
—and you, hostess. He is very sick and would to bed.
Good Bardolph, put thy face between his sheets and
do the office of a warming pan. Faith, he's very ill.

Bard. Away, you rogue!   85

Host. By my troth, he'll yield the crow a pudding

88. **presently:** at once.

98. **manhood shall compound:** prowess shall decide; i.e., it depends on who is the victor; **Push home:** i.e., do your worst.

101-2. **"Sword" is an oath:** that is, a sword was often used to swear by, as in *Hamlet*, I. [v.], because the hilt and blade formed a cross; **must have their course:** must be submitted to.

103. **an:** if.

108. **A noble:** a gold coin worth six and a half shillings; **present:** immediate.

111. **Nym:** a pun, since "nim" means "steal."

112. **sutler:** provisioner to the army.

one of these days. The King has killed his heart. Good
husband, come home presently.   *Exit.*

Bard. Come, shall I make you two friends? We
must to France together. Why the devil should we   90
keep knives to cut one another's throats?

Pist. Let floods o'erswell, and fiends for food howl
on!

Nym. You'll pay me the eight shillings I won of you
at betting?   95

Pist. Base is the slave that pays.

Nym. That now I will have. That's the humor of it.

Pist. As manhood shall compound. Push home.

                                            They draw.

Bard. By this sword, he that makes the first thrust,
I'll kill him! By this sword, I will.   [*Draws.*] 100

Pist. "Sword" is an oath, and oaths must have their
    course.   [*Sheathes his sword.*]

Bard. Corporal Nym, an thou wilt be friends, be
friends; an thou wilt not, why then be enemies with
me too. Prithee put up.   105

Nym. I shall have my eight shillings I won of you
at betting?

Pist. A noble shalt thou have, and present pay;
And liquor likewise will I give to thee,
And friendship shall combine, and brotherhood.   110
I'll live by Nym, and Nym shall live by me.
Is not this just? For I shall sutler be
Unto the camp, and profits will accrue.
Give me thy hand.

                            [*Nym sheathes his sword.*]

120. **quotidian tertian:** the Hostess runs together the names of a fever occurring daily (**quotidian**) and one occurring every other day (**tertian**).

122. **hath run bad humors on the knight:** has pushed the knight into a state of low spirits.

125. **fracted and corroborate:** broken; a malapropism by Pistol, who likes big words even though he misuses them.

127. **passes some humors and careers:** indulges in some rather capricious actions. To "pass a career" was a term from horsemanship meaning to gallop at top speed for a short stretch.

128. **condole:** condole with.

[II. ii.] King Henry is aware of the treason of Scroop, Cambridge, and Grey, and tests them by asking their opinion of the punishment he should deal out to a man who criticized himself while drunk. He wishes to be merciful, particularly since the culprit is repentant now that he is sober, but the three traitors urge a harsh penalty. Henry nevertheless orders the man's release. Cambridge, Scroop, and Grey are given papers supposedly containing their commissions but actually setting forth the discovery of their treason. All three express their repentance and joy that their treasonous purpose has been prevented, before they are led away to execution.

This unpleasant business finished, the King cheerfully prepares to set sail for France.

4. **even:** calmly.

Nym. I shall have my noble?   115
Pist. In cash, most justly paid.
Nym. Well then, that's the humor of't.

                          Enter *Hostess.*

Host. As ever you come of women, come in quickly
to Sir John. Ah, poor heart! he is so shaked of a burn-
ing quotidian tertian that it is most lamentable to be-   120
hold. Sweet men, come to him.
Nym. The King hath run bad humors on the knight;
that's the even of it.
Pist. Nym, thou hast spoke the right.
His heart is fracted and corroborate.   125
Nym. The King is a good king, but it must be as it
may. He passes some humors and careers.
Pist. Let us condole the knight; for, lambkins, we
  will live.

                                            Exeunt.

[Scene II. Southampton. A council chamber.]

  Enter *Exeter, Bedford,* and *Westmoreland.*

Bed. Fore God, his Grace is bold to trust these
  traitors.
Exe. They shall be apprehended by-and-by.
West. How smooth and even they do bear themselves,   5

10. **his bedfellow:** i.e., Scroop, as Henry's words at ll. 105 ff. indicate.

22. **in head:** organized as an army.

26. **That grows not in a fair consent with ours:** is not in full emotional agreement with us; see I. [ii.] 187 and 213.

As if allegiance in their bosoms sat,
Crowned with faith and constant loyalty!
  Bed. The King hath note of all that they intend,
By interception which they dream not of.
  Exe. Nay, but the man that was his bedfellow,   10
Whom he hath dulled and cloyed with gracious
      favors—
That he should, for a foreign purse, so sell
His sovereign's life to death and treachery!

Sound trumpets. Enter the *King, Scroop, Cambridge,*
      and *Grey,* [*Lords,* and *Attendants*].

  King. Now sits the wind fair, and we will aboard.   15
My Lord of Cambridge, and my kind Lord of
      Masham,
And you, my gentle knight, give me your thoughts.
Think you not that the pow'rs we bear with us
Will cut their passage through the force of France,   20
Doing the execution and the act
For which we have in head assembled them?
  Scroop. No doubt, my liege, if each man do his best.
  King. I doubt not that, since we are well persuaded
We carry not a heart with us from hence   25
That grows not in a fair consent with ours,
Nor leave not one behind that doth not wish
Success and conquest to attend on us.
  Cam. Never was monarch better feared and loved
Than is your Majesty. There's not, I think, a subject 30
That sits in heart-grief and uneasiness
Under the sweet shade of your government.

34. **steeped their galls in honey:** sweetened their grievances as though they had been dipped in honey.

35. **create:** fully composed.

38. **the office of our hand:** that is, how to use our hands.

39. **quittance:** full payment.

45. **Enlarge:** release.

46. **railed against:** criticized.

48. **his more advice:** his sober reconsideration.

49. **security:** confidence in safety.

51. **his sufferance:** the merciful treatment of him; the toleration of his action.

58. **heavy orisons:** weighty appeals.

59. **proceeding on distemper:** stemming from intoxication.

60. **stretch our eye:** i.e., open our eyes wide in horror.

61-2. **capital crimes:** crimes meriting punishment by death; **chewed, swallowed, and digested:** i.e., the criminals have not suffered revulsion on further consideration, but have been able to stomach capital crimes.

Grey. True. Those that were your father's enemies
Have steeped their galls in honey and do serve you
With hearts create of duty and of zeal.   35

King. We therefore have great cause of thankful-
    ness,
And shall forget the office of our hand
Sooner than quittance of desert and merit
According to the weight and worthiness.   40

Scroop. So service shall with steeled sinews toil,
And labor shall refresh itself with hope,
To do your Grace incessant services.

King. We judge no less. Uncle of Exeter,
Enlarge the man committed yesterday   45
That railed against our person. We consider
It was excess of wine that set him on,
And on his more advice, we pardon him.

Scroop. That's mercy, but too much security.
Let him be punished, sovereign, lest example   50
Breed (by his sufferance) more of such a kind.

King. O let us yet be mercifull

Cam. So may your Highness, and yet punish too.

Grey. Sir,
You show great mercy if you give him life   55
After the taste of much correction.

King. Alas, your too much love and care of me
Are heavy orisons 'gainst this poor wretch!
If little faults proceeding on distemper
Shall not be winked at, how shall we stretch our eye   60
When capital crimes, chewed, swallowed, and di-
    gested,

84. **cowarded:** made cowards of.
89. **quick:** alive.

Appear before us? We'll yet enlarge that man,
Though Cambridge, Scroop, and Grey, in their dear
    care   65
And tender preservation of our person,
Would have him punished. And now to our French
    causes.
Who are the late commissioners?
  Cam. I one, my lord.   70
Your Highness bade me ask for it today.
  Scroop. So did you me, my liege.
  Grey. And I, my royal sovereign.
  King. Then, Richard Earl of Cambridge, there is
    yours;   75
There yours, Lord Scroop of Masham; and, Sir Knight,
Grey of Northumberland, this same is yours.
Read them, and know I know your worthiness.
My Lord of Westmoreland, and uncle Exeter,
We will aboard tonight.—Why how now, gentlemen?   80
What see you in those papers that you lose
So much complexion?—Look ye, how they change!
Their cheeks are paper.—Why, what read you there
That hath so cowarded and chased your blood
Out of appearance?   85
  Cam.   I do confess my fault,
And do submit me to your Highness' mercy.
  Grey, Scroop. To which we all appeal.
  King. The mercy that was quick in us but late,
By your own counsel is suppressed and killed.   90
You must not dare (for shame) to talk of mercy;
For your own reasons turn into your bosoms
As dogs upon their masters, worrying you.

97. **accord:** agree.

98. **appertinents:** appurtenances, furnishings.

101. **practices:** plots.

110. **Wouldst thou have practiced on me for thy use:** if you had made use of me to suit your purposes.

113. **annoy:** harm.

114. **gross:** evident, clear.

118-19. **Working so grossly in a natural cause/ That admiration did not whoop at them:** so obviously employed in a cause suiting their natures that their behavior provoked no wonder.

120. **'gainst all proportion:** in a most unnatural fashion.

121. **wait on:** escort; see I. i. 102.

123. **wrought upon thee so preposterously:** worked on you so monstrously.

124. **voice:** reputation.

See you, my princes and my noble peers,
These English monsters! My Lord of Cambridge 95
     here—
You know how apt our love was to accord
To furnish him with all appertinents
Belonging to his honor; and this man
Hath, for a few light crowns, lightly conspired 100
And sworn unto the practices of France
To kill us here in Hampton; to the which
This knight, no less for bounty bound to us
Than Cambridge is, hath likewise sworn. But O,
What shall I say to thee, Lord Scroop, thou cruel, 105
Ingrateful, savage, and inhuman creature?
Thou that didst bear the key of all my counsels,
That knewst the very bottom of my soul,
That (almost) mightst have coined me into gold,
Wouldst thou have practiced on me for thy use— 110
May it be possible that foreign hire
Could out of thee extract one spark of evil
That might annoy my finger? 'Tis so strange
That, though the truth of it stands off as gross
As black and white, my eye will scarcely see it. 115
Treason and murder ever kept together,
As two yoke-devils sworn to either's purpose,
Working so grossly in a natural cause
That admiration did not whoop at them;
But thou ('gainst all proportion) didst bring in 120
Wonder to wait on treason and on murder;
And whatsoever cunning fiend it was
That wrought upon thee so preposterously
Hath got the voice in hell for excellence,

125. **suggest:** tempt.

126-28. **botch . . . piety:** clumsily cover a damnable deed with a patchwork covering of nobility.

129. **tempered thee:** molded you to his own use; **bade thee stand up:** ordered you to range yourself on his side with full knowledge of the nature of his cause, like a powerful lord, soliciting your allegiance and promising no reward but the title "traitor."

132. **gulled:** duped, misled.

133. **with his lion gait:** "your adversary the devil, as a roaring lion, walketh about, seeking whom he may devour," I Pet. 5:8.

134. **Tartar:** Tartarus, the classical name for hell.

135. **legions:** hosts of demons; see Mark 5:9.

137. **jealousy:** suspicion.

138. **affiance:** pledged faith.

143. **gross . . . anger:** strong feelings of gaiety or anger.

144. **swerving:** shifting; **blood:** impulse.

145. **modest complement:** the appearance of calm temperance.

146. **Not . . . ear:** not acting on the evidence of sight without confirmation by additional knowledge.

147. **but in purged judgment trusting neither:** i.e., trusting neither without first having resolved all doubts. **Purged** means cleansed or purified.

148. **finely bolted:** well sifted; clear of defects.

150. **full-fraught . . . and best-indued:** completely laden and best endowed (with virtues).

154. **to the answer of the law:** to answer the legal charges against them.

155. **acquit:** pardon; **of:** for; **practices:** plots.

And other devils that suggest by treasons   125
Do botch and bungle up damnation
With patches, colors, and with forms being fetched
From glist'ring semblances of piety;
But he that tempered thee bade thee stand up,
Gave thee no instance why thou shouldst do treason, 130
Unless to dub thee with the name of traitor.
If that same demon that hath gulled thee thus
Should with his lion gait walk the whole world,
He might return to vasty Tartar back
And tell the legions, "I can never win   135
A soul so easy as that Englishman's."
O how hast thou with jealousy infected
The sweetness of affiance! Show men dutiful?
Why, so didst thou. Seem they grave and learned?
Why, so didst thou. Come they of noble family?   140
Why, so didst thou. Seem they religious?
Why, so didst thou. Or are they spare in diet,
Free from gross passion or of mirth or anger,
Constant in spirit, not swerving with the blood,
Garnished and decked in modest complement,   145
Not working with the eye without the ear,
And but in purged judgment trusting neither?
Such and so finely bolted didst thou seem;
And thus thy fall hath left a kind of blot
To mark the full-fraught man and best indued   150
With some suspicion. I will weep for thee;
For this revolt of thine, methinks, is like
Another fall of man. Their faults are open.
Arrest them to the answer of the law;
And God acquit them of their practices!   155

162. **discovered:** revealed.
170. **sufferance:** endurance of the punishment.
182. **golden earnest:** token payment of gold to
seal the bargain.

Exe. I arrest thee of high treason by the name of
Richard Earl of Cambridge.

I arrest thee of high treason by the name of Henry
Lord Scroop of Masham.

I arrest thee of high treason by the name of Thomas 160
Grey, knight, of Northumberland.

Scroop. Our purposes God justly hath discovered,
And I repent my fault more than my death,
Which I beseech your Highness to forgive,
Although my body pay the price of it.   165

Cam. For me, the gold of France did not seduce,
Although I did admit it as a motive
The sooner to effect what I intended.
But God be thanked for prevention,
Which I in sufferance heartily will rejoice,   170
Beseeching God, and you, to pardon me.

Grey. Never did faithful subject more rejoice
At the discovery of most dangerous treason
Than I do at this hour joy o'er myself,
Prevented from a damned enterprise.   175
My fault, but not my body, pardon, sovereign.

King. God quit you in his mercy! Hear your sen-
    tence.
You have conspired against our royal person,
Joined with an enemy proclaimed, and from his 180
    coffers
Received the golden earnest of our death;
Wherein you would have sold your king to slaughter,
His princes and his peers to servitude,
His subjects to oppression and contempt,   185
And his whole kingdom into desolation.

188. **tender:** cherish.

194. **dear:** grievous.

201. **rub:** a bowling term: obstacle.

204. **straight:** immediately; **in expedition:** under speedy way.

205. **Cheerly to sea:** with good cheer, let us put to sea; **the signs of war advance:** raise our battle standards.

▬▬▬▬▬▬▬▬▬▬▬▬▬▬▬▬▬▬▬▬

[II. iii.] Pistol, Bardolph, the Hostess, and Nym mourn the death of Falstaff as the men set off for war.

▬▬▬▬▬▬▬▬▬▬▬▬▬▬

1. **bring:** escort.

2. **Staines:** a village on the Thames on the route to Southampton.

3. **earn:** yearn, mourn.

Touching our person, seek we no revenge,
But we our kingdom's safety must so tender,
Whose ruin you have sought, that to her laws
We do deliver you. Get you therefore hence   190
(Poor miserable wretches) to your death;
The taste whereof God of his mercy give
You patience to endure, and true repentance
Of all your dear offenses! Bear them hence.

    Exeunt [Cambridge, Scroop, and Grey, guarded].
Now, lords, for France; the enterprise whereof   195
Shall be to you as us, like glorious.
We doubt not of a fair and lucky war,
Since God so graciously hath brought to light
This dangerous treason, lurking in our way
To hinder our beginnings. We doubt not now   200
But every rub is smoothed on our way.
Then, forth, dear countrymen. Let us deliver
Our puissance into the hand of God,
Putting it straight in expedition.
Cheerly to sea; the signs of war advance.   205
No king of England, if not King of France!

                    Flourish. Exeunt.

[Scene III. London. A tavern.]

Enter *Pistol, Nym, Bardolph, Boy,* and *Hostess.*

    Host. Prithee, honey-sweet husband, let me bring
thee to Staines.
    Pist. No; for my manly heart doth earn.

4. **rouse thy vaunting veins:** raise up your habitual spirit of braggadocio.

10. **Arthur's bosom:** possibly the Hostess' error for "Abraham's bosom"; **'A:** he.

12. **christom child:** newly-christened child; i.e., he died peacefully; **parted:** departed.

17. **babbled:** first suggested by Lewis Theobald to correct the Folio reading "table." This is one of the most famous and highly praised emendations in Shakespeare. But recently the passage has become the subject of controversy. Professor Leslie Hotson would retain the reading "table," meaning "picture," and maintains that "green fields" indicates that Falstaff is thinking of the hero Richard Grenville, whose name Hotson asserts was pronounced "Greenfield." Theobald's emendation is not likely to be replaced.

27. **of:** i.e., against; **sack:** sherry.

Bardolph, be blithe; Nym, rouse thy vaunting veins;
Boy, bristle thy courage up; for Falstaff he is dead,   5
And we must earn therefore.

Bard. Would I were with him, wheresome'er he is,
either in heaven or in hell!

Host. Nay sure, he's not in hell! He's in Arthur's
bosom, if ever man went to Arthur's bosom. 'A made   10
a finer end, and went away an it had been any
christom child. 'A parted ev'n just between twelve
and one, ev'n at the turning o' the tide. For after I
saw him fumble with the sheets, and play with
flowers, and smile upon his finger's end, I knew there   15
was but one way; for his nose was as sharp as a pen,
and 'a babbled of green fields. "How now, Sir John?"
quoth I. "What, man? be o' good cheer." So 'a cried
out "God, God, God!" three or four times. Now I, to
comfort him, bid him 'a should not think of God; I   20
hoped there was no need to trouble himself with any
such thoughts yet. So 'a bade me lay more clothes on
his feet. I put my hand into the bed and felt them,
and they were as cold as any stone. Then I felt to his
knees, and so upward and upward, and all was as cold   25
as any stone.

Nym. They say he cried out of sack.

Host. Ay, that 'a did.

Bard. And of women.

Host. Nay, that 'a did not.   30

Boy. Yes, that 'a did, and said they were devils in-
carnate.

Host. 'A could never abide carnation; 'twas a color
he never liked.

35-6. **about women:** that is, because of his weakness for women.

37. **handle:** deal with verbally, refer to; with a double meaning.

38. **rheumatic:** probably a pun, unintentional on the Hostess' part, on the pronunciation "Rome-atic." Preaching against the "Whore of Babylon" was a feature of anti-Catholic sentiment. The Hostess very likely meant some synonym for "delirious."

43. **the fuel:** i.e., the liquor drunk at Falstaff's expense, which reddened Bardolph's nose.

45. **shog:** be off; see [II. i.] 45.

49. **Let senses rule:** be ruled by your common sense; **The word is "Pitch and pay":** let your motto be: "Nothing on the cuff."

51. **wafer cakes:** pastry, which is easily broken.

52. **Holdfast is the only dog:** a proverbial expression: Brag is a good dog, but Holdfast is better. In other words, keep a firm grip on all valuable possessions.

53. **Caveto:** caution, from the Latin *caveo*.

54. **clear thy crystals:** wipe your eyes.

62. **Let housewifery appear. Keep close:** show your thrift. Keep all safe.

Boy. 'A said once the devil would have him about 35
women.

Host. 'A did in some sort, indeed, handle women;
but then he was rheumatic, and talked of the Whore
of Babylon.

Boy. Do you not remember 'a saw a flea stick upon 40
Bardolph's nose, and 'a said it was a black soul burn-
ing in hell?

Bard. Well, the fuel is gone that maintained that
fire. That's all the riches I got in his service.

Nym. Shall we shog? The King will be gone from 45
Southampton.

Pist. Come, let's away. My love, give me thy lips.
Look to my chattels and my movables.
Let senses rule. The word is "Pitch and pay."
Trust none;   50
For oaths are straws, men's faiths are wafer cakes,
And Holdfast is the only dog, my duck.
Therefore Caveto be thy counselor.
Go, clear thy crystals. Yoke-fellows in arms,
Let us to France, like horseleeches, my boys,   55
To suck, to suck, the very blood to suck!

Boy. And that's but unwholesome food, they say.

Pist. Touch her soft mouth, and march.

Bard. Farewell, hostess.   [*Kisses her.*]

Nym. I cannot kiss, that is the humor of it; but 60
adieu!

Pist. Let housewifery appear. Keep close, I thee
    command.

Host. Farewell! adieu!

                                            Exeunt.

[II. iv.] The French King and his chief officers make preparations to repel the English invasion. The Dauphin is still scornful of Henry's threat and sees no danger to France, but nonetheless agrees that it is sensible to prepare. The council of war is interrupted by the arrival of English ambassadors. They present a genealogical table setting forth King Henry's claim to the French crown and the threat that he will seize it if he cannot gain it peaceably.

▬▬▬▬▬▬▬▬▬▬▬▬▬▬▬▬

Ent. **Britaine:** i.e., Bretagne.

8. **line:** reinforce.

9. **means defendant:** defensive means.

11. **gulf:** whirlpool.

13. **late examples:** the English victories at Crécy and Poitiers.

14. **fatal and neglected:** i.e., deadly because underestimated.

16. **redoubted:** formidable, feared.

17. **meet:** fitting; see I. [ii.] 264.

22. **As were a war:** as if a war were.

[Scene IV. France. The King's Palace.]

Flourish. Enter the *French King,* the *Dauphin,* the *Dukes of Berri* and *Britaine,* [the *Constable,* and others].

   King. Thus comes the English with full power upon us,
And more than carefully it us concerns
To answer royally in our defenses.
Therefore the Dukes of Berri and Britaine,   5
Of Brabant and of Orleans, shall make forth,
And you, Prince Dauphin, with all swift dispatch,
To line and new repair our towns of war
With men of courage and with means defendant;
For England his approaches makes as fierce   10
As waters to the sucking of a gulf.
It fits us then to be as provident
As fear may teach us out of late examples
Left by the fatal and neglected English
Upon our fields.   15
   Dau.   My most redoubted father,
It is most meet we arm us 'gainst the foe;
For peace itself should not so dull a kingdom
(Though war nor no known quarrel were in question)
But that defenses, musters, preparations   20
Should be maintained, assembled, and collected,
As were a war in expectation.
Therefore I say 'tis meet we all go forth
To view the sick and feeble parts of France;

27. **Whitsun morris dance:** a dance in costume, featuring such characters as Robin Hood and Maid Marian, and usually a hobbyhorse, which was performed during the celebration of Whitsuntide.

28. **so idly kinged:** ruled by so frivolous a monarch.

29. **Her scepter so fantastically borne:** governed so capriciously.

30. **vain:** worthless; **humorous:** capricious; see humors [II. i.] 127.

31. **attends her not:** i.e., is no part of her company.

37. **How modest in exception:** how temperately he replied to the Dauphin's insulting message; see modest [II. ii.] 145.

39. **his vanities forespent:** the foolish behavior of his past life.

40. **the Roman Brutus:** Lucius Junius Brutus, known as Brutus the Liberator because he took part in the overthrow of the Tarquins in Rome. He concealed his serious intent from his uncle Tarquinius Superbus by pretending to be mentally deficient.

42. **ordure:** excrement, fertilizer.

48. **the proportions of defense are filled:** the necessary military forces are supplied.

49. **of a weak and niggardly projection:** planned to an inadequate and miserly scale.

50. **scanting:** saving.

54. **hath been fleshed upon us:** have already tasted our flesh (so that King Henry will have inherited a taste for it). The metaphor is from hunting; hounds, as well as hawks, were trained to hunt by being given a taste of the flesh of the quarry.

55. **strain:** breed.

And let us do it with no show of fear—   25
No, with no more than if we heard that England
Were busied with a Whitsun morris dance;
For, my good liege, she is so idly kinged,
Her scepter so fantastically borne,
By a vain, giddy, shallow, humorous youth,   30
That fear attends her not.

    Con.   O peace, Prince Dauphin!
You are too much mistaken in this king.
Question your Grace the late ambassadors,
With what great state he heard their embassy,   35
How well supplied with noble counselors,
How modest in exception, and withal
How terrible in constant resolution,
And you shall find his vanities forespent
Were but the outside of the Roman Brutus,   40
Covering discretion with a coat of folly;
As gardeners do with ordure hide those roots
That shall first spring and be most delicate.

    Dau. Well, 'tis not so, my Lord High Constable!
But though we think it so, it is no matter.   45
In cases of defense 'tis best to weigh
The enemy more mighty than he seems.
So the proportions of defense are filled;
Which of a weak and niggardly projection
Doth, like a miser, spoil his coat with scanting   50
A little cloth.

    King.   Think we King Harry strong;
And, princes, look you strongly arm to meet him.
The kindred of him hath been fleshed upon us;
And he is bred out of that bloody strain   55

Edward III.
From John Taylor, *All the Works* (1630).

56. haunted: pursued.

58. struck: fought.

61. mountain sire: great sire; i.e., Edward III. Shakespeare is using the word in a double sense; Edward III was born in the mountains of Wales.

68. native mightiness and fate of him: the great destiny which his birth assures him.

71. present: immediate.

78. Take up the English short: i.e., make short work of them.

That haunted us in our familiar paths.
Witness our too much memorable shame
When Crécy battle fatally was struck,
And all our princes captived, by the hand
Of that black name, Edward, Black Prince of Wales;   60
Whiles that his mountain sire—on mountain standing,
Up in the air, crowned with the golden sun—
Saw his heroical seed, and smiled to see him,
Mangle the work of nature, and deface
The patterns that by God and by French fathers   65
Had twenty years been made. This is a stem
Of that victorious stock; and let us fear
The native mightiness and fate of him.

Enter a *Messenger.*

Mess. Ambassadors from Harry King of England
Do crave admittance to your Majesty.   70
    King. We'll give them present audience. Go, and
        bring them.
            [*Exeunt Messenger and certain Lords.*]
You see this chase is hotly followed, friends.
    Dau. Turn head, and stop pursuit; for coward dogs
Most spend their mouths when what they seem to   75
        threaten
Runs far before them. Good my sovereign,
Take up the English short, and let them know
Of what a monarchy you are the head.
Self-love, my liege, is not so vile a sin   80
As self-neglecting.

90. **the ordinance of times:** long-established law.

92. **sinister:** illegitimate; **awkward:** irregular, perverse; almost synonymous with **sinister**.

95. **line:** table of descent, pedigree.

96. **truly demonstrative:** offering accurate proof.

98. **evenly:** justly, correctly.

101-3. **indirectly held/ From:** wrongly kept from; **native and true challenger:** true claimant by right of birth; see **native**, l. 68.

108. **requiring:** requesting, mere asking.

Charles VI, King of France.
From H. C., *Abbrege de l'histoire françoise* (1596).

Enter [*Lords,* with] *Exeter* [and *Train*].

King.   From our brother of England?
Exe. From him, and thus he greets your Majesty:
He wills you, in the name of God Almighty,
That you devest yourself, and lay apart   85
The borrowed glories that by gift of heaven,
By law of nature and of nations, 'longs
To him and to his heirs—namely, the crown
And all wide-stretched honors that pertain
By custom, and the ordinance of times,   90
Unto the crown of France. That you may know
'Tis no sinister nor no awkward claim,
Picked from the wormholes of long-vanished days,
Nor from the dust of old oblivion raked,
He sends you this most memorable line,   95

                              [*Gives a paper.*]
In every branch truly demonstrative;
Willing you overlook this pedigree;
And when you find him evenly derived
From his most famed of famous ancestors,
Edward the Third, he bids you then resign   100
Your crown and kingdom, indirectly held
From him, the native and true challenger.
    King. Or else what follows?
    Exe. Bloody constraint; for if you hide the crown
Even in your hearts, there will he rake for it.   105
Therefore in fierce tempest is he coming,
In thunder and in earthquake, like a Jove;
That, if requiring fail, he will compel;

109. **in the bowels of the Lord:** by the mercy of God.

114. **'prived:** suggested by J. H. Walter. The Folio reads "priuy," the Quarto "pining."

128. **An if:** if.

134. **second accent:** echo; **ordinance:** cannon.

139. **Paris balls:** tennis balls.

And bids you, in the bowels of the Lord,
Deliver up the crown, and to take mercy　　　　　　110
On the poor souls for whom this hungry war
Opens his vasty jaws; and on your head
Turning the widows' tears, the orphans' cries,
The dead men's blood, the 'prived maidens' groans,
For husbands, fathers, and betrothed lovers　　　　115
That shall be swallowed in this controversy.
This is his claim, his threat'ning, and my message;
Unless the Dauphin be in presence here,
To whom expressly I bring greeting too.

   King. For us, we will consider of this further.　　120
Tomorrow shall you bear our full intent
Back to our brother England.

   Dau.　　　　　　　　　　For the Dauphin,
I stand here for him. What to him from England?

   Exe. Scorn and defiance, slight regard, contempt,　　125
And anything that may not misbecome
The mighty sender, doth he prize you at.
Thus says my king: An if your father's Highness
Do not, in grant of all demands at large,
Sweeten the bitter mock you sent his Majesty,　　130
He'll call you to so hot an answer of it
That caves and womby vaultages of France
Shall chide your trespass, and return your mock
In second accent of his ordinance.

   Dau. Say, if my father render fair return,　　135
It is against my will; for I desire
Nothing but odds with England. To that end,
As matching to his youth and vanity,
I did present him with the Paris balls.

140. Louvre: a pun on "lover"; the Folio text spells the word "louer."

Phoebus, the sun god.
From Vincenzo Cartari, *Imagini de gli dei delli antichi* (1615).

Exe. He'll make your Paris Louvre shake for it,   140
Were it the mistress court of mighty Europe;
And be assured you'll find a difference,
As we his subjects have in wonder found,
Between the promise of his greener days
And these he masters now. Now he weighs time   145
Even to the utmost grain. That you shall read
In your own losses, if he stay in France.
    King. Tomorrow shall you know our mind at full.
    Exe. Dispatch us with all speed, lest that our king
Come here himself to question our delay;   150
For he is footed in this land already.
    King. You shall be soon dispatched with fair condi-
      tions.
A night is but small breath and little pause
To answer matters of this consequence.   155
                      Flourish. Exeunt.

THE LIFE OF
KING HENRY
THE FIFTH

ACT III

Cho. [III.] The Chorus describes the sailing of King Henry's magnificent fleet from Southampton, with the flower of English manhood. The ambassadors to the French King have brought back the offer of the hand of his daughter Katherine in marriage and some minor territories; this being far short of Henry's demands, Harfleur is now besieged.

1. **imagined wing:** wings of imagination.
2. **celerity:** speed.
4. **Hampton:** Southampton. The Folio reads "Dover," by Shakespeare's time the normal port of embarkation for France. Theobald made the correction, since the Chorus has clearly indicated Southampton as the sailing point.
5. **brave:** fine; a compliment to the appearance, not the valor, of the fleet.
6. **silken streamers:** i.e., flags; **the young Phoebus fanning:** fluttering in the face of the early-morning sun.
7. **Play:** i.e., take part in the performance.
10. **threaden:** woven of thread.
14. **rivage:** banks.
18. **Grapple your minds to sternage of this navy:** follow the navy with your minds as though they were grappled to the ships' sterns.
21. **pith:** synonymous with **puissance;** strength.

ACT [III]

Enter *Chorus*.

Thus with imagined wing our swift scene flies,
In motion of no less celerity
Than that of thought. Suppose that you have seen
The well-appointed King at Hampton pier
Embark his royalty; and his brave fleet   5
With silken streamers the young Phoebus fanning.
Play with your fancies; and in them behold
Upon the hempen tackle shipboys climbing;
Hear the shrill whistle, which doth order give
To sounds confused; behold the threaden sails,   10
Borne with the invisible and creeping wind,
Draw the huge bottoms through the furrowed sea,
Breasting the lofty surge. O, do but think
You stand upon the rivage and behold
A city on the inconstant billows dancing;   15
For so appears this fleet majestical,
Holding due course to Harfleur. Follow, follow!
Grapple your minds to sternage of this navy,
And leave your England as dead midnight still,
Guarded with grandsires, babies, and old women,   20
Either past or not arrived to pith and puissance;

39

24. **culled and choice-drawn:** weeded out and selected one by one; i.e., carefully hand picked.

27. **girded:** surrounded, besieged.

30. **to dowry:** as dowry.

32. **likes:** pleases.

33. **linstock:** a long stick used to light cannon.

S.D. after l. 33. **Alarum:** the sound of a trumpet as a call to battle; **chambers:** probably here small ordnance used in the playhouse for sound effects.

[**III. i.**] King Henry and his troops are storming Harfleur, and the King makes a rousing speech exhorting his men to show the French the mettle of Englishmen.

Gunner lighting a cannon with a linstock.
From an 1869 reprint of Edward Webbe, *The Rare and Most Wonderful Things* (1590).

40

For who is he whose chin is but enriched
With one appearing hair that will not follow
These culled and choice-drawn cavaliers to France?
Work, work your thoughts, and therein see a siege.   25
Behold the ordinance on their carriages,
With fatal mouths gaping on girded Harfleur.
Suppose the ambassador from the French comes back;
Tells Harry that the King doth offer him
Katherine his daughter, and with her to dowry   30
Some petty and unprofitable dukedoms.
The offer likes not; and the nimble gunner
With linstock now the devilish cannon touches,
                    Alarum, and chambers go off.
And down goes all before them. Still be kind,
And eke out our performance with your mind.   35
                              Exit.

[Scene I. France. Before Harfleur.]

Alarum. Enter the *King, Exeter, Bedford,* and
Gloucester, [and *Soldiers* with] scaling ladders
            at Harfleur.

King. Once more unto the breach, dear friends,
    once more;
Or close the wall up with our English dead!
In peace there's nothing so becomes a man
As modest stillness and humility;   5
But when the blast of war blows in our ears,

8. **summon:** Nicholas Rowe's correction of the Folio's "commune."

9. **fair nature:** your naturally kindly expressions; **hard-favored:** harsh-visaged, stern-faced.

11. **portage of the head:** i.e., eyesockets.

12. **o'erwhelm:** overhang.

13. **galled:** chafed; worn away by erosion and the action of the waves.

14. **jutty:** synonymous with **o'erhang; confounded:** destroyed; i.e., the part washed away by the ocean.

15. **Swilled:** possibly two meanings: drenched, and greedily swallowed, gulped.

17-8. **bend up every spirit/ To his full height:** strain every power to the limit.

19. **fet:** fetched, derived; **fathers of war-proof:** fathers whose valor has been demonstrated.

22. **for lack of argument:** i.e., only because there was no further opposition.

23. **attest:** confirm.

25. **copy:** example.

28. **mettle of your pasture:** quality of your breeding.

33. **slips:** leashes.

34. **Straining:** Rowe's correction of the Folio "straying"; **Straining upon the start:** straining in eagerness to start.

35. **upon this charge:** while charging.

Then imitate the action of the tiger:
Stiffen the sinews, summon up the blood,
Disguise fair nature with hard-favored rage;
Then lend the eye a terrible aspect;   10
Let it pry through the portage of the head
Like the brass cannon; let the brow o'erwhelm it
As fearfully as doth a galled rock
O'erhang and jutty his confounded base,
Swilled with the wild and wasteful ocean.   15
Now set the teeth and stretch the nostril wide,
Hold hard the breath and bend up every spirit
To his full height! On, on, you noblest English,
Whose blood is fet from fathers of war-proof!
Fathers that like so many Alexanders   20
Have in these parts from morn till even fought,
And sheathed their swords for lack of argument.
Dishonor not your mothers; now attest
That those whom you called fathers did beget you!
Be copy now to men of grosser blood   25
And teach them how to war! And you, good yeomen,
Whose limbs were made in England, show us here
The mettle of your pasture. Let us swear
That you are worth your breeding; which I doubt
    not,   30
For there is none of you so mean and base
That hath not noble luster in your eyes.
I see you stand like greyhounds in the slips,
Straining upon the start. The game's afoot!
Follow your spirit; and upon this charge   35
Cry "God for Harry! England and Saint George!"
            [*Exeunt.*] *Alarum, and chambers go off.*

[III. ii.] The "sworn brothers" and the boy are discovered enduring the fighting with some discomfort, but Captain Fluellen drives them back into battle when they attempt to avoid it. Captains Fluellen, a Welshman, Macmorris, an Irishman, and Jamy, a Scot, discuss the proper conduct of military operations.

---

4. **case:** set.

5-6. **very plain song:** plain and simple truth. Plain song is a simple tune without variations.

7-8. **humors do abound:** i.e., there's too much going on.

18. **hie:** hurry.

19. **duly, but not as truly:** exactly and truly, yet not truly in the sense of faithfully, since he would be deserting his allegiance to the King.

21. **Avaunt:** be off.

22. **cullions:** contemptible rascals.

Scaling ladders at a siege.
From Olaus Magnus, *Historia de gentibus septentrionalibus* (1555).

42

[Scene II. Before Harfleur.]

Enter *Nym, Bardolph, Pistol,* and *Boy.*

Bard. On, on, on, on, on! to the breach, to the
breach!

Nym. Pray thee, Corporal, stay. The knocks are
too hot; and, for mine own part, I have not a case of
lives. The humor of it is too hot; that is the very plain   5
song of it.

Pist. The plain song is most just; for humors do
    abound.

Knocks go and come; God's vassals drop and die;
            And sword and shield   10
            In bloody field
            Doth win immortal fame.

Boy. Would I were in an alehouse in London! I
would give all my fame for a pot of ale and safety.

Pist. And I: 15

        If wishes would prevail with me,
        My purpose should not fail with me,
          But thither would I hie,
Boy.   As duly, but not as truly,
          As bird doth sing on bough.   20

Enter *Fluellen.*

Flu. Up to the breach, you dogs! Avaunt, you
cullions!   [*Drives them forward.*]

23. **men of mold:** earthly creatures, mortals.

26. **bawcock:** fine fellow, from the French *beau coq*.

28-9. **These be good humors. Your honor wins bad humors:** i.e., Pistol's words make sense; Fluellen's forcing them back into battle goes against the grain.

31. **swashers:** swashbucklers; phony heroes; **boy:** i.e., he is younger and their servant.

33. **antics:** buffoons.

49. **carry coals:** be capable of any low action and show little courage. The occupation of delivering coals was held in contempt.

Pist. Be merciful, great duke, to men of mold!
Abate thy rage, abate thy manly rage,
Abate thy rage, great duke!   25
Good bawcock, 'bate thy rage! Use lenity, sweet
    chuck!

Nym. These be good humors. Your honor wins
bad humors.   *Exit [with all except Boy.]*

Boy. As young as I am, I have observed these   30
three swashers. I am boy to them all three; but all
they three, though they would serve me, could not
be man to me; for indeed three such antics do not
amount to a man. For Bardolph, he is white-livered
and red-faced; by the means whereof 'a faces it out,   35
but fights not. For Pistol, he hath a killing tongue
and a quiet sword; by the means whereof 'a breaks
words and keeps whole weapons. For Nym, he hath
heard that men of few words are the best men, and
therefore he scorns to say his prayers, lest 'a should   40
be thought a coward; but his few bad words are
matched with as few good deeds, for 'a never broke
any man's head but his own, and that was against a
post when he was drunk. They will steal anything,
and call it purchase. Bardolph stole a lute-case, bore   45
it twelve leagues, and sold it for three halfpence.
Nym and Bardolph are sworn brothers in filching,
and in Calais they stole a fire-shovel. I knew by that
piece of service the men would carry coals. They
would have me as familiar with men's pockets as   50
their gloves or their handkerchers; which makes
much against my manhood, if I should take from an-

62. **disciplines of the war:** proper military practice.

65. **is digt himself four yard under the countermines:** has himself dug countermines four yards under our mines.

66. **plow:** blow. Fluellen is given a dialectal speech throughout.

68. **order:** ordering, management.

73. **an ass, as in the world:** as big an ass as there is.

74-5. **verify as much in his beard:** prove as much to his face; **directions:** command.

other's pocket to put into mine; for it is plain pocketing up of wrongs. I must leave them and seek some better service. Their villainy goes against my weak 55 stomach, and therefore I must cast it up.   *Exit.*

Enter *Gower* [and *Fluellen*].

Gow. Captain Fluellen, you must come presently to the mines. The Duke of Gloucester would speak with you.

Flu. To the mines? Tell you the Duke, it is not so 60 good to come to the mines; for look you, the mines is not according to the disciplines of the war. The concavities of it is not sufficient; for look you, the athversary, you may discuss unto the Duke, look you, is digt himself four yard under the countermines. By 65 Cheshu, I think 'a will plow up all, if there is not better directions.

Gow. The Duke of Gloucester, to whom the order of the siege is given, is altogether directed by an Irishman, a very valiant gentleman, i' faith. 70

Flu. It is Captain Macmorris, is it not?

Gow. I think it be.

Flu. By Cheshu, he is an ass, as in the world! I will verify as much in his beard. He has no more directions in the true disciplines of the wars, look you, of 75 the Roman disciplines, than is a puppy dog.

Enter *Macmorris* and *Captain Jamy*.

Gow. Here 'a comes, and the Scots captain, Captain Jamy, with him.

80. **expedition:** readiness to discuss theory; a rhetorical term.

84. **pristine:** early.

87. **God-den:** good day.

90. **pioners:** pioneers, miners.

98. **voutsafe:** vouchsafe, allow; **a few disputations:** a short discussion.

107. **marry:** by the Virgin Mary.

Flu. Captain Jamy is a marvelous falorous gentleman, that is certain, and of great expedition and   80
knowledge in the aunchient wars, upon my particular knowledge of his directions. By Cheshu, he will
maintain his argument as well as any military man
in the world in the disciplines of the pristine wars
of the Romans.   85

Jamy. I say gud day, Captain Fluellen.

Flu. God-den to your worship, good Captain
James.

Gow. How now, Captain Macmorris? Have you
quit the mines? Have the pioners given o'er?   90

Mac. By Chrish, law, tish ill done! The work ish
give over, the trompet sound the retreat. By my
hand I swear, and my father's soul, the work ish ill
done! It ish give over. I would have blowed up the
town, so Chrish save me law! in an hour. O, tish ill   95
done! tish ill done! By my hand, tish ill done!

Flu. Captain Macmorris, I beseech you now, will
you voutsafe me, look you, a few disputations with
you, as partly touching or concerning the disciplines
of the war, the Roman wars? In the way of argu-   100
ment, look you, and friendly communication; partly
to satisfy my opinion, and partly for the satisfaction,
look you, of my mind—as touching the direction of
the military discipline, that is the point.

Jamy. It sall be vary gud, gud feith, gud Captens   105
bath, and I sall quit you with gud leve, as I may
pick occasion. That sall I, marry.

Mac. It is no time to discourse, so Chrish save me!
The day is hot, and the weather, and the wars, and

111. **beseeched:** besieged.

112. **be:** by.

117. **mess:** mass.

123-24. **under your correction:** correct me if I am wrong.

137. **you will mistake each other:** will is emphatic: you are bent upon misunderstanding each other.

Besieging a town.
From Olaus Magnus, *Historia de gentibus septentrionalibus* (1555).

the King, and the Dukes. It is no time to discourse. 110
The town is beseeched, and the trompet call us to
the breach, and we talk, and, be Chrish, do nothing.
'Tis shame for us all. So God sa' me, 'tis shame to
stand still, it is shame, by my hand! and there is
throats to be cut, and works to be done, and there 115
ish nothing done, so Chrish sa' me, law!

Jamy. By the mess, ere theise eyes of mine take
themselves to slomber, I'll de gud service, or I'll lig
i' the grund for it! ay, or go to death! And I'll pay't
as valorously as I may, that sall I suerly do, that is 120
the breff and the long. Marry, I wad full fain heard
some question 'tween you tway.

Flu. Captain Macmorris, I think, look you, under
your correction, there is not many of your nation—

Mac. Of my nation? What ish my nation? Ish a 125
villain, and a bastard, and a knave, and a rascal.
What ish my nation? Who talks of my nation?

Flu. Look you, if you take the matter otherwise
than is meant, Captain Macmorris, peradventure I
shall think you do not use me with that affability 130
as in discretion you ought to use me, look you, being
as good a man as yourself, both in the disciplines of
war, and in the derivation of my birth, and in other
particularities.

Mac. I do not know you so good a man as myself. 135
So Chrish save me, I will cut off your head!

Gow. Gentlemen both, you will mistake each other.

Jamy. Ah, that's a foul fault!

                                    A parley [sounded].

Gow. The town sounds a parley.

141. **to be required:** available for the asking.

━━━━━━━━━━━━━━━━━━━━━━━━━━━━━━

[III. iii.] King Henry threatens the governor of Harfleur with complete destruction of the town and all the attendant horrors of a sacking unless he surrenders. The governor replies that the Dauphin is unable to relieve the town and he has no choice except to surrender. The King leaves Harfleur in the command of the Earl of Exeter while he retires with the main body of his troops to rest at Calais.

━━━━━━━━━━━━━━━━━━━━━━━━━━━━━━

4. **proud of destruction:** exultant at the thought of death.

8. **half-achieved:** half-conquered.

11. **fleshed:** hardened and bloodthirsty; see [II. iv.] 54.

12. **In liberty of bloody hand shall range:** shall roam at large with no restraint on his bloody deeds.

17. **fell:** fierce, savage.

Flu. Captain Macmorris, when there is more bet- 140
ter opportunity to be required, look you, I will be so
bold as to tell you I know the disciplines of war; and
there is an end.

Exeunt.

[Scene III. Before the gates of Harfleur.]

Enter *King* [*Henry*] and all his *Train* before the
gates.

King. How yet resolves the governor of the town?
This is the latest parle we will admit.
Therefore to our best mercy give yourselves,
Or, like to men proud of destruction,
Defy us to our worst; for, as I am a soldier,
A name that in my thoughts becomes me best,
If I begin the batt'ry once again,
I will not leave the half-achieved Harfleur
Till in her ashes she lie buried.
The gates of mercy shall be all shut up,   10
And the fleshed soldier, rough and hard of heart,
In liberty of bloody hand shall range
With conscience wide as hell, mowing like grass
Your fresh fair virgins and your flow'ring infants.
What is it then to me if impious war,   15
Arrayed in flames like to the prince of fiends,
Do with his smirched complexion all fell feats
Enlinked to waste and desolation?
What is't to me, when you yourselves are cause,

23. **career:** headlong gallop; see [II. i.] 127.

24. **bootless:** vainly.

26. **precepts:** written commands.

30. **grace:** mercy.

32. **heady:** headstrong.

34. **blind:** bereft of all discrimination; uncontrolled.

41. **Herod's bloody-hunting slaughtermen:** a reference to the slaughter of the innocents; see Matt. 2:16.

43. **guilty in defense:** guilty of failing to surrender at the point demanded by the contemporary laws of war, if complete sack of the city were to be prevented.

46. **Returns us:** replies.

If your pure maidens fall into the hand   20
Of hot and forcing violation?
What rein can hold licentious wickedness
When down the hill he holds his fierce career?
We may as bootless spend our vain command
Upon the enraged soldiers in their spoil   25
As send precepts to the Leviathan
To come ashore. Therefore, you men of Harfleur,
Take pity of your town and of your people
Whiles yet my soldiers are in my command,
Whiles yet the cool and temperate wind of grace   30
O'erblows the filthy and contagious clouds
Of heady murder, spoil, and villainy.
If not—why, in a moment look to see
The blind and bloody soldier with foul hand
Defile the locks of your shrill-shrieking daughters; 35
Your fathers taken by the silver beards,
And their most reverend heads dashed to the walls;
Your naked infants spitted upon pikes,
Whiles the mad mothers with their howls confused
Do break the clouds, as did the wives of Jewry   40
At Herod's bloody-hunting slaughtermen.
What say you? Will you yield, and this avoid?
Or, guilty in defense, be thus destroyed?

            Enter *Governor* [on the wall].

  Gov. Our expectation hath this day an end.
The Dauphin, whom of succors we entreated,   45
Returns us that his powers are yet not ready
To raise so great a siege. Therefore, great king,

55. **For us:** that is, as for me.

59. **address:** prepared.

▬▬▬▬▬▬▬▬▬▬▬▬▬▬▬▬▬▬▬▬▬▬

[III. iv.] Katherine, daughter of the French King, takes a lesson in English from one of her attendants.

The point of this passage is to provide comedy. Katherine confuses English words with French words of similar sound which in some instances have indecent connotations.

▬▬▬▬▬▬▬▬▬▬▬▬▬▬▬▬▬▬

Henry V.
From John Taylor, *All the Works* (1630).

We yield our town and lives to thy soft mercy.
Enter our gates, dispose of us and ours,
For we no longer are defensible. 50
King. Open your gates.   [*Exit Governor.*]
                    Come, uncle Exeter,
Go you and enter Harfleur, there remain
And fortify it strongly 'gainst the French.
Use mercy to them all. For us, dear uncle, 55
The winter coming on, and sickness growing
Upon our soldiers, we will retire to Calais.
Tonight in Harfleur will we be your guest;
Tomorrow for the march are we addrest.
          Flourish, and enter the town.

[Scene IV. Rouen. The King's Palace.]

Enter *Katherine* and [*Alice,*] an old *Gentlewoman.*

Kath. Alice, tu as été en Angleterre, et tu parles
bien le langage.
Alice. Un peu, madame.
Kath. Je te prie m'enseigner; il faut que j'apprenne
à parler. Comment appelez-vous la main en Anglais? 5
Alice. La main? Elle est appelée "de hand."
Kath. "De hand." Et les doigts?
Alice. Les doigts? Ma foi, j'oublie les doigts; mais
je me souviendrai. Les doigts? Je pense qu'ils sont
appelés "de fingres"; oui, "de fingres." 10
Kath. La main, "de hand"; les doigts, "de fingres."
Je pense que je suis le bon écolier; j'ai gagné deux

mots d'Anglais vitement. Comment appelez-vous les ongles?

Alice. Les ongles? Nous les appelons "de nails."   15

Kath. "De nails." Écoutez; dites-moi, si je parle bien: "de hand, de fingres," et "de nails."

Alice. C'est bien dit, madame; il est fort bon Anglais.

Kath. Dites-moi l'Anglais pour le bras.   20

Alice. "De arm," madame.

Kath. Et le coude.

Alice. "D'elbow."

Kath. "D'elbow." Je m'en fais la répétition de tous les mots que vous m'avez appris dès à présent.   25

Alice. Il est trop difficile, madame, comme je pense.

Kath. Excusez-moi, Alice; écoutez: "d'hand, de fingres, de nails, d'arma, de bilbow."

Alice. "D'elbow," madame.   30

Kath. O Seigneur Dieu, je m'en oublie! "D'elbow." Comment appelez-vous le col?

Alice. "De nick," madame.

Kath. "De nick." Et le menton?

Alice. "De chin."   35

Kath. "De sin." Le col, "de nick"; le menton, "de sin."

Alice. Oui. Sauf votre honneur, en vérité, vous prononcez les mots aussi droit que les natifs d'Angleterre.   40

Kath. Je ne doute point d'apprendre, par la grace de Dieu, et en peu de temps.

[III. v.] The French King, the Dauphin, and their lords decide that it is time to stop Henry's progress through France. A herald is sent to ask the English King what ransom he will give for his own safety.

Alice. N'avez-vous pas déjà oublié ce que je vous
ai enseigné?

Kath. Non, je réciterai à vous promptement: 45
"d'hand, de fingres, de mails"—

Alice. "De nails," madame.

Kath. "De nails, de arm, de ilbow."

Alice. Sauf votre honneur, "d'elbow."

Kath. Ainsi dis-je; "d'elbow, de nick," et "de sin." 50
Comment appelez-vous le pied et la robe?

Alice. "De foot," madame; et "de coun."

Kath. "Le foot" et "le count"! O Seigneur Dieu!
ils sont mots de son mauvais, corruptible, gros et
impudique, et non pour les dames d'honneur d'user: 55
je ne voudrais prononcer ces mots devant les sei-
gneurs de France pour tout le monde. Foh! "le foot"
et "le count"! Néanmoins, je réciterai une autre fois
ma leçon ensemble: "d'hand, de fingre, de nails,
d'arm, d'elbow, de nick, de sin, de foot, le count." 60

Alice. Excellent, madame!

Kath. C'est assez pour une fois: allons-nous à diner.
Exeunt.

[Scene V. Rouen. The Palace.]

Enter the *King of France*, the *Dauphin*, [*Britaine*,]
the *Constable of France*, and others.

King. 'Tis certain he hath passed the river Somme.
Con. And if he be not fought withal, my lord,

5. **Dieu vivant:** by the living God; **a few sprays of us:** that is, a few offshoots of French blood.

6. **luxury:** lust.

8. **Spirt:** spurt, shoot up like a plant.

12. **Mort de ma vie:** literally, death of my life.

13. **but:** that is, I will sell my dukedom unless our forces attack the English.

14. **slobbery:** slimy, muddy.

15. **nook-shotten:** set in a remote corner; spoken in the same spirit as we might speak of a Godforsaken place; **Albion:** England.

16. **Dieu de batailles:** God of battles.

20. **sodden:** boiled.

21. **drench:** draught; **sur-reined:** overridden; **jades:** a contemptuous term for horses; **barley broth:** i.e., ale, which was used in treating horses in England.

22. **Decoct:** warm.

28. **"Poor":** that is, the rich fields in l. 27 have worthless owners.

Let us not live in France; let us quit all
And give our vineyards to a barbarous people.
   Dau. O Dieu vivant! Shall a few sprays of us,   5
The emptying of our fathers' luxury,
Our scions, put in wild and savage stock,
Spirt up so suddenly into the clouds
And overlook their grafters?
   Brit. Normans, but bastard Normans, Norman 10
    bastards!
Mort de ma vie! if they march along
Unfought withal, but I will sell my dukedom
To buy a slobbery and a dirty farm
In that nook-shotten isle of Albion.   15
   Con. Dieu de batailles! whence have they this
    mettle?
Is not their climate foggy, raw, and dull,
On whom, as in despite, the sun looks pale,
Killing their fruit with frowns? Can sodden water, 20
A drench for sur-reined jades, their barley broth,
Decoct their cold blood to such valiant heat?
And shall our quick blood, spirited with wine,
Seem frosty? O, for honor of our land,
Let us not hang like roping icicles   25
Upon our houses' thatch, whiles a more frosty people
Sweat drops of gallant youth in our rich fields—
"Poor" we may call them in their native lords!
   Dau. By faith and honor,
Our madams mock at us and plainly say   30
Our mettle is bred out, and they will give
Their bodies to the lust of English youth
To new-store France with bastard warriors.

35. **lavoltas:** dances with leaping steps; **corantos:** dances with running step.

36. **grace:** virtue, noteworthy ability.

37. **lofty runaways:** a pun on the distinguishing characteristics of the two dances already referred to.

50. **seats:** feudal holdings; i.e., your positions as great lords of France; **quit you:** acquit yourselves.

55. **rheum:** phlegm.

64. **for achievement:** in place of a victory; i.e., instead of fighting.

Brit. They bid us to the English dancing schools
And teach lavoltas high and swift corantos,   35
Saying our grace is only in our heels
And that we are most lofty runaways.
    King. Where is Montjoy the herald? Speed him
        hence;
Let him greet England with our sharp defiance.   40
Up, princes! and, with spirit of honor edged,
More sharper than your swords, hie to the field.
Charles Delabreth, High Constable of France,
You Dukes of Orleans, Bourbon, and of Berri,
Alençon, Brabant, Bar, and Burgundy;   45
Jaques Chatillon, Rambures, Vaudemont,
Beaumont, Grandpré, Roussi, and Faulconbridge,
Foix, Lestrale, Bouciqualt, and Charolois,
High dukes, great princes, barons, lords, and knights,
For your great seats now quit you of great shames.   50
Bar Harry England, that sweeps through our land
With pennons painted in the blood of Harfleur.
Rush on his host as doth the melted snow
Upon the valleys whose low vassal seat
The Alps doth spit and void his rheum upon.   55
Go down upon him—you have power enough—
And in a captive chariot into Rouen
Bring him our prisoner.
    Con.   This becomes the great.
Sorry am I his numbers are so few,   60
His soldiers sick and famished in their march;
For I am sure, when he shall see our army,
He'll drop his heart into the sink of fear
And, for achievement, offer us his ransom.

[III. vi.] Fluellen has been praising the valor of Pistol to Captain Gower when Pistol himself enters to ask Fluellen's assistance in gaining a pardon for Bardolph, who has been sentenced to hang for robbing a church. Fluellen refuses to intercede in what he considers a just penalty and Pistol leaves in a rage.

The French Herald comes to the King to ask what ransom he is prepared to pay for his safety. Henry replies that he is not at the moment seeking battle but will not avoid it if the French present themselves. He scornfully rejects the idea of ransoming himself.

6. **magnanimous:** great in courage.

King. Therefore, Lord Constable, haste on 65
Montjoy,
And let him say to England that we send
To know what willing ransom he will give.
Prince Dauphin, you shall stay with us in Rouen.
Dau. Not so, I do beseech your Majesty. 70
King. Be patient, for you shall remain with us.
Now forth, Lord Constable and princes all,
And quickly bring us word of England's fall.

Exeunt.

[Scene VI. The English camp in Picardy.]

Enter *Captains*, English and Welsh—*Gower* and
Fluellen.

Gow. How now, Captain Fluellen? Come you from
the bridge?
Flu. I assure you there is very excellent services
committed at the bridge.
Gow. Is the Duke of Exeter safe? 5
Flu. The Duke of Exeter is as magnanimous as
Agamemnon, and a man that I love and honor with
my soul, and my heart, and my duty, and my live,
and my living, and my uttermost power. He is not—
God be praised and plessed!—any hurt in the world, 10
but keeps the pridge most valiantly, with excellent
discipline. There is an aunchient lieutenant there at
the pridge, I think in my very conscience he is as
valiant a man as Mark Antony, and he is a man of no

15. **estimation:** reputation.

40. **pax:** a small tablet containing a picture of the Crucifixion which was passed around to be kissed by communicants during Mass.

The mutable goddess Fortune.
From Andrea Alciati, *Emblemata* (1584).

estimation in the world, but I did see him do as gal-   15
lant service.

Gow. What do you call him?

Flu. He is called Aunchient Pistol.

Gow. I know him not.

Enter *Pistol.*

Flu. Here is the man.   20

Pist. Captain, I thee beseech to do me favors.
The Duke of Exeter doth love thee well.

Flu. Ay, I praise God; and I have merited some
love at his hands.

Pist. Bardolph, a soldier firm and sound of heart,   25
And of buxom valor, hath by cruel fate,
And giddy Fortune's furious fickle wheel—
That goddess blind,
That stands upon the rolling restless stone—

Flu. By your patience, Aunchient Pistol. Fortune is   30
painted plind, with a muffler afore her eyes, to signify
to you that Fortune is plind; and she is painted also
with a wheel, to signify to you, which is the moral
of it, that she is turning and inconstant, and mutabil-
ity, and variation; and her foot, look you, is fixed   35
upon a spherical stone, which rolls, and rolls, and
rolls. In good truth, the poet makes a most excellent
description of it. Fortune is an excellent moral.

Pist. Fortune is Bardolph's foe, and frowns on him;
For he hath stol'n a pax, and hanged must 'a be—   40
A damned death!
Let gallows gape for dog; let man go free,
And let not hemp his windpipe suffocate.

57, 60. **figo . . . The fig of Spain**: obscene terms of contempt, usually accompanied by a gesture with the thumb and forefinger.

62. **arrant**: absolute, unqualified.

67. **when time is serve**: i.e., when opportunity offers he will be revenged.

72. **learn you by rote**: learn by heart.

73. **sconce**: earthwork.

But Exeter hath given the doom of death
For pax of little price. 45
Therefore, go speak—the Duke will hear thy voice;
And let not Bardolph's vital thread be cut
With edge of penny cord and vile reproach.
Speak, Captain, for his life, and I will thee requite.

Flu. Aunchient Pistol, I do partly understand your 50
meaning.

Pist. Why then, rejoice therefore!

Flu. Certainly, aunchient, it is not a thing to rejoice
at; for if, look you, he were my brother, I would desire the Duke to use his good pleasure and put him to 55
execution; for discipline ought to be used.

Pist. Die and be damned! and figo for thy friendship!

Flu. It is well.

Pist. The fig of Spain! *Exit.* 60

Flu. Very good.

Gow. Why, this is an arrant counterfeit rascal! I remember him now—a bawd, a cutpurse.

Flu. I'll assure you, 'a utt'red as prave words at the
pridge as you shall see in a summer's day. But it is 65
very well. What he has spoke to me, that is well, I
warrant you, when time is serve.

Gow. Why, 'tis a gull, a fool, a rogue, that now and
then goes to the wars to grace himself, at his return
into London, under the form of a soldier. And such 70
fellows are perfect in the great commanders' names,
and they will learn you by rote where services were
done:—at such and such a sconce, at such a breach,
at such a convoy; who came off bravely, who was

76. **con:** learn.
77. **new-tuned:** in the latest fashion.
81. **slanders:** disgracers, scandals.
85. **a hole in his coat:** that is, a flaw in the false front he presents; an opportunity to shame him.
87. **from the pridge:** about the bridge.
99. **perdition:** loss of life.

shot, who disgraced, what terms the enemy stood on; 75
and this they con perfectly in the phrase of war,
which they trick up with new-tuned oaths; and what
a beard of the General's cut and a horrid suit of the
camp will do among foaming bottles and ale-washed
wits is wonderful to be thought on. But you must 80
learn to know such slanders of the age, or else you
may be marvelously mistook.

Flu. I tell you what, Captain Gower, I do perceive
he is not the man that he would gladly make show
to the world he is. If I find a hole in his coat, I will tell 85
him my mind. [*Drum within.*] Hark you, the King is
coming, and I must speak with him from the pridge.

Drum and colors. Enter the *King* and his poor
Soldiers [and *Gloucester*].

God pless your Majesty!
King. How now, Fluellen? Camest thou from the
   bridge? 90
Flu. Ay, so please your Majesty. The Duke of
Exeter has very gallantly maintained the pridge; the
French is gone off, look you, and there is gallant and
most prave passages. Marry, the athversary was have
possession of the pridge, but he is enforced to retire, 95
and the Duke of Exeter is master of the pridge. I can
tell your Majesty, the Duke is a prave man.
King. What men have you lost, Fluellen?
Flu. The perdition of the athversary hath been
very great, reasonable great. Marry, for my part, I 100
think the Duke hath lost never a man but one that is
like to be executed for robbing a church—one Bar-

104. **bubukles:** Fluellen combines "bubo" (abscess) and "carbuncle"; **whelks:** pimples.

Ent. after l. 114. **Tucket:** the sound of a trumpet.

115. **habit:** uniform, livery.

116. **of:** from.

122. **Advantage:** favorable opportunity; see I. [ii.] 144.

124-25. **bruise:** squeeze, as might be done to a pus-filled swelling; **were full ripe:** had come to a head.

126. **England:** that is, the English King.

127. **admire:** wonder at; **sufferance:** tolerance, forbearance; see [II. ii.] 51.

128. **proportion:** i.e., be proportioned according to.

130-31. **digested:** had to stomach; see **digest,** [II. ii.] 61-2; **in weight to re-answer, his pettiness would bow under:** i.e., his means are too slight to make full recompense for.

dolph, if your Majesty know the man. His face is all
bubukles and whelks, and knobs, and flames o' fire,
and his lips blows at his nose, and it is like a coal of 105
fire, sometimes plue and sometimes red; but his nose
is executed, and his fire's out.

King. We would have all such offenders so cut off.
And we give express charge that in our marches
through the country there be nothing compelled from 110
the villages, nothing taken but paid for; none of the
French upbraided or abused in disdainful language;
for when lenity and cruelty play for a kingdom, the
gentler gamester is the soonest winner.

Tucket. Enter Montjoy.

Mont. You know me by my habit. 115

King. Well then, I know thee. What shall I know of
thee?

Mont. My master's mind.

King. Unfold it.

Mont. Thus says my king:—Say thou to Harry of 120
England: Though we seemed dead, we did but sleep.
Advantage is a better soldier than rashness. Tell him
we could have rebuked him at Harfleur, but that we
thought not good to bruise an injury till it were full
ripe. Now we speak upon our cue, and our voice is 125
imperial. England shall repent his folly, see his weakness, and admire our sufferance. Bid him therefore
consider of his ransom, which must proportion the
losses we have borne, the subjects we have lost, the
disgrace we have digested; which in weight to re- 130
answer, his pettiness would bow under. For our losses,

133. **muster:** i.e., all the inhabitants.
145. **impeachment:** hindrance, obstruction; **sooth:** truth.
147. **vantage:** advantage, as in l. 122.
157. **trunk:** body.

his exchequer is too poor; for the effusion of our
blood, the muster of his kingdom too faint a number;
and for our disgrace, his own person kneeling at our
feet but a weak and worthless satisfaction. To this add 135
defiance; and tell him for conclusion he hath be-
trayed his followers, whose condemnation is pronounced. So far my king and master; so much my
office.

King. What is thy name? I know thy quality. 140
Mont. Montjoy.
King. Thou dost thy office fairly. Turn thee back,
And tell thy king I do not seek him now,
But could be willing to march on to Calais
Without impeachment: for, to say the sooth, 145
Though 'tis no wisdom to confess so much
Unto an enemy of craft and vantage,
My people are with sickness much enfeebled,
My numbers lessened, and those few I have,
Almost no better than so many French; 150
Who when they were in health, I tell thee, herald,
I thought upon one pair of English legs
Did march three Frenchmen. Yet forgive me, God,
That I do brag thus! This your air of France
Hath blown that vice in me. I must repent. 155
Go therefore tell thy master here I am;
My ransom is this frail and worthless trunk;
My army but a weak and sickly guard;
Yet, God before, tell him we will come on,
Though France himself and such another neighbor 160
Stand in our way. There's for thy labor, Montjoy.
                                        [*Gives a purse.*]

162. **well advise himself:** consider carefully; see
I. [ii.] 185 and 261.

▬▬▬▬▬▬▬▬▬▬▬▬▬▬▬▬

[III. vii.] The French prepare for the morrow's
battle. The Dauphin, in high spirits, expecting a
rout of the English, extols the virtues of his horse;
he and other French lords wonder at the stupidity
of the English at coming thus to be slaughtered.

▬▬▬▬▬▬▬▬▬▬▬▬▬▬

Bellerophon on Pegasus, slaying the Chimera.
From Andrea Alciati, *Emblemata* (1584).
(See [III. vii.] 14.)

Go bid thy master well advise himself:
If we may pass, we will; if we be hind'red,
We shall your tawny ground with your red blood
Discolor; and so, Montjoy, fare you well.   165
The sum of all our answer is but this:
We would not seek a battle, as we are,
Nor, as we are, we say we will not shun it.
So tell your master.

    Mont. I shall deliver so. Thanks to your Highness. 170
                                      [Exit.]

    Glouc. I hope they will not come upon us now.
    King. We are in God's hand, brother, not in theirs.
March to the bridge. It now draws toward night.
Beyond the river we'll encamp ourselves,
And on tomorrow bid them march away.   175

                                  Exeunt.

[Scene VII. The French camp, near Agincourt.]

Enter the *Constable of France,* the *Lord Rambures,*
    Orleans, Dauphin, with others.

    Con. Tut! I have the best armor of the world.
Would it were day!
    Orl. You have an excellent armor; but let my horse
have his due.
    Con. It is the best horse of Europe.   5
    Orl. Will it never be morning?
    Dau. My Lord of Orleans, and my Lord High Con-
stable, you talk of horse and armor?

12. **pasterns:** literally, part of the horse's feet; used loosely here for hoofs.

13-5. **as if his entrails were hairs:** i.e., with the resilience of a tennis ball, the stuffing of which was hair; **le cheval volant:** the flying horse; **Pegasus:** the winged horse born of the Gorgon Medusa's blood when she was killed by Perseus; **avec les narines de feu:** with nostrils of fire. Perhaps Shakespeare confused his recollection of the adventures of Perseus and Bellerophon, both of whom are connected with the horse Pegasus. It was Bellerophon, riding on Pegasus, who slew the Chimera, a dragon with three heads, one of which breathed fire. The passage may only describe the horse's high spirit, however.

18. **the pipe of Hermes:** Hermes (Mercury) was supposed to have invented the shepherd's pipe or syrinx.

25. **absolute:** flawless.

27. **palfreys:** critics have pointed out that a palfrey is a lady's saddle horse instead of a war horse and Shakespeare may have used the term to suggest the Dauphin's effeminate taste. The next line, however, attributes to the horse warlike qualities, which suggests that **palfrey** may be simply a careless error.

32-3. **vary . . . praise on:** praise with variations on a literary theme.

35. **argument:** subject of discussion.

Orl. You are as well provided of both as any prince
in the world.   10

Dau. What a long night is this! I will not change
my horse with any that treads but on four pasterns.
Ça, ha! he bounds from the earth, as if his entrails
were hairs; le cheval volant, the Pegasus, avec les
narines de feu! When I bestride him, I soar, I am a   15
hawk. He trots the air. The earth sings when he
touches it. The basest horn of his hoof is more musical
than the pipe of Hermes.

Orl. He's of the color of the nutmeg.

Dau. And of the heat of the ginger. It is a beast for   20
Perseus: he is pure air and fire; and the dull elements
of earth and water never appear in him, but only in
patient stillness while his rider mounts him. He is indeed a horse, and all other jades you may call beasts.

Con. Indeed, my lord, it is a most absolute and   25
excellent horse.

Dau. It is the prince of palfreys. His neigh is like
the bidding of a monarch, and his countenance enforces homage.

Orl. No more, cousin.   30

Dau. Nay, the man hath no wit that cannot, from
the rising of the lark to the lodging of the lamb, vary
deserved praise on my palfrey. It is a theme as fluent
as the sea. Turn the sands into eloquent tongues, and
my horse is argument for them all. 'Tis a subject for a   35
sovereign to reason on, and for a sovereign's sovereign
to ride on; and for the world, familiar to us and un-
known, to lay apart their particular functions and

46. **prescript:** prescribed.

47. **particular:** exclusively one's own.

49. **shrewdly:** ill-naturedly, maliciously.

52. **belike:** most likely.

53-4. **kern:** actually a foot soldier; **your French hose off, and in your strait strossers.** French hose were full breeches, which did not reach to the knee and were supplemented by long stockings. The Irish kerns are pictured in John Derricke's *Image of Ireland* (1581) as wearing a jerkin-like garment but no breeches, and sometimes no hose. See illustration on page 63. **Strossers** means trousers.

59. **jade:** a worthless horse; see l. 24; and a loose woman.

64-5. **Le chien est retourné à son propre vomissement, et la truie lavée au bourbier:** "the dog is turned to his own vomit again; and the sow that was washed to her wallowing in the mire," II Pet. 2:22.

wonder at him. I once writ a sonnet in his praise and
began thus, "Wonder of nature!"   40

Orl. I have heard a sonnet begin so to one's
mistress.

Dau. Then did they imitate that which I composed
to my courser, for my horse is my mistress.

Orl. Your mistress bears well.   45

Dau. Me well, which is the prescript praise and
perfection of a good and particular mistress.

Con. Nay, for methought yesterday your mistress
shrewdly shook your back.

Dau. So perhaps did yours.   50

Con. Mine was not bridled.

Dau. O, then belike she was old and gentle, and
you rode like a kern of Ireland, your French hose off,
and in your strait strossers.

Con. You have good judgment in horsemanship.   55

Dau. Be warned by me then. They that ride so, and
ride not warily, fall into foul bogs. I had rather have
my horse to my mistress.

Con. I had as lief have my mistress a jade.

Dau. I tell thee, Constable, my mistress wears his   60
own hair.

Con. I could make as true a boast as that, if I had a
sow to my mistress.

Dau. "Le chien est retourné à son propre vomissement, et la truie lavée au bourbier." Thou makest use   65
of anything.

Con. Yet do I not use my horse for my mistress,
or any such proverb so little kin to the purpose.

An Irish kern.
From an 1883 reprint of John Derricke, *The Image of Ireland*
(1581).

82-3. **faced out of my way:** forced to a shameful
retreat.

85. **go to hazard with me:** i.e., wager with me.
Hazard is the name of a dice game.

99. **still:** always.

Ram. My Lord Constable, the armor that I saw in
your tent tonight--are those stars or suns upon it?   70

Con. Stars, my lord.

Dau. Some of them will fall tomorrow, I hope.

Con. And yet my sky shall not want.

Dau. That may be, for you bear a many superflu-
ously, and 'twere more honor some were away.   75

Con. Ev'n as your horse bears your praises, who
would trot as well, were some of your brags dis-
mounted.

Dau. Would I were able to load him with his
desert! Will it never be day? I will trot tomorrow a   80
mile, and my way shall be paved with English faces.

Con. I will not say so, for fear I should be faced
out of my way; but I would it were morning, for I
would fain be about the ears of the English.

Ram. Who will go to hazard with me for twenty   85
prisoners?

Con. You must first go yourself to hazard ere you
have them.

Dau. 'Tis midnight; I'll go arm myself.   *Exit.*

Orl. The Dauphin longs for morning.   90

Ram. He longs to eat the English.

Con. I think he will eat all he kills.

Orl. By the white hand of my lady, he's a gallant
prince.

Con. Swear by her foot, that she may tread out the   95
oath.

Orl. He is simply the most active gentleman of
France.

Con. Doing is activity, and he will still be doing.

110-12. Never anybody saw it but his lackey: i.e., he has never displayed it except in striking his body servant; **a hooded valor; and when it appears, it will bate:** he keeps his courage under wraps most of the time (as a hawk was hooded to calm it) and when he reveals it, it soon ebbs away. There is a pun on "abate" and "bate" (the fluttering of a hawk's wings when it is alarmed or distressed, as when first unhooded and set on the prey).

123. shot over: overshot the mark.

124. overshot: outshot, defeated in a shooting match.

Orl. He never did harm, that I heard of.   100

Con. Nor will do none tomorrow. He will keep that good name still.

Orl. I know him to be valiant.

Con. I was told that by one that knows him better than you.   105

Orl. What's he?

Con. Marry, he told me so himself, and he said he cared not who knew it.

Orl. He needs not; it is no hidden virtue in him.

Con. By my faith, sir, but it is! Never anybody saw   110
it but his lackey. 'Tis a hooded valor; and when it appears, it will bate.

Orl. Ill will never said well.

Con. I will cap that proverb with "There is flattery in friendship."   115

Orl. And I will take up that with "Give the Devil his due."

Con. Well placed! There stands your friend for the Devil. Have at the very eye of that proverb with "A pox of the Devil!"   120

Orl. You are the better at proverbs, by how much "a fool's bolt is soon shot."

Con. You have shot over.

Orl. 'Tis not the first time you were overshot.

Enter a *Messenger.*

Mess. My Lord High Constable, the English lie   125
within fifteen hundred paces of your tents.

Con. Who hath measured the ground?

Mess. The Lord Grandpré.

132. peevish: childish, foolish.

133-34. to mope with his fat-brained followers so far out of his knowledge: to stray dreamily with his stupid followers so far from familiar country that he is in danger of becoming lost; i.e., he is not fully conscious of where he is going, the hazard he is incurring.

135. apprehension: grasp of the situation.

142. Foolish curs: an allusion to the popular sport of bearbaiting with trained mastiffs.

146. sympathize with: i.e., act in accord with.

151. shrewdly: distressingly, grievously.

An armorer at work.
From Hartmann Schopper, *Panoplia omnium illiberalium* (1568).
(See Cho. [IV.] 12.)

Con. A valiant and most expert gentleman. Would it were day! Alas, poor Harry of England! He longs 130 not for the dawning, as we do.

Orl. What a wretched and peevish fellow is this King of England, to mope with his fat-brained followers so far out of his knowledge!

Con. If the English had any apprehension, they 135 would run away.

Orl. That they lack; for if their heads had any intellectual armor, they could never wear such heavy headpieces.

Ram. That island of England breeds very valiant 140 creatures. Their mastiffs are of unmatchable courage.

Orl. Foolish curs, that run winking into the mouth of a Russian bear and have their heads crushed like rotten apples! You may as well say that's a valiant flea that dare eat his breakfast on the lip of a lion. 145

Con. Just, just! and the men do sympathize with the mastiffs in robustious and rough coming on, leaving their wits with their wives; and then give them great meals of beef and iron and steel, they will eat like wolves and fight like devils. 150

Orl. Ay, but these English are shrewdly out of beef.

Con. Then shall we find tomorrow they have only stomachs to eat and none to fight. Now is it time to arm. Come, shall we about it?

Orl. It is now two o'clock; but let me see—by ten 155 We shall have each a hundred Englishmen.

Exeunt.

THE LIFE OF
KING HENRY
THE FIFTH

ACT IV

Cho. [IV.] The Chorus describes the night before the battle, with the flickering of campfires, the neighing of horses, and the sound of the armorers putting equipment in order. King Henry moves among his troops cheering the dispirited.

▬▬▬▬▬▬▬▬▬▬▬

1. **entertain conjecture:** allow yourselves to imagine, or picture.

2. **poring:** i.e., requiring **poring** (intent peering) to be penetrated.

5. **stilly sounds:** is audible in the stillness of the night.

8. **paly:** i.e., palelike; having the effect of dividing by vertical uprights.

9. **battle:** army; **umbered:** darkened, shadowed.

12. **accomplishing:** finishing the armor of.

17. **secure:** overconfident; see **security,** [II. ii.] 49.

18. **overlusty:** overgay.

19. **play at dice:** i.e., wagering them as prisoners; see [III. vii.] 85.

ACT [IV]

Chorus.

Now entertain conjecture of a time
When creeping murmur and the poring dark
Fills the wide vessel of the universe.
From camp to camp, through the foul womb of night,
The hum of either army stilly sounds,   5
That the fixed sentinels almost receive
The secret whispers of each other's watch.
Fire answers fire, and through their paly flames
Each battle sees the other's umbered face.
Steed threatens steed, in high and boastful neighs   10
Piercing the night's dull ear; and from the tents
The armorers accomplishing the knights,
With busy hammers closing rivets up,
Give dreadful note of preparation.
The country cocks do crow, the clocks do toll   15
And the third hour of drowsy morning name.
Proud of their numbers and secure in soul,
The confident and overlusty French
Do the low-rated English play at dice;
And chide the cripple tardy-gaited night   20

25. **gesture sad:** grave air.

26. **Investing:** clothing.

37-8. **dedicate one jot of color/ Unto the weary and all-watched night:** i.e., he is not pale despite the weary night during which he has not slept.

39. **overbears attaint:** suppresses the effect of exhaustion.

43. **largess:** freely offered benefit.

44. **liberal:** generous.

45. **mean and gentle all:** everyone, plebeian and gentleman alike.

46. **as may unworthiness define:** if the unworthy speaker may describe it thus.

Who like a foul and ugly witch doth limp
So tediously away. The poor condemned English,
Like sacrifices, by their watchful fires
Sit patiently and inly ruminate
The morning's danger; and their gesture sad,   25
Investing lank-lean cheeks and war-worn coats,
Presenteth them unto the gazing moon
So many horrid ghosts. O now, who will behold
The royal captain of this ruined band
Walking from watch to watch, from tent to tent,   30
Let him cry "Praise and glory on his head!"
For forth he goes and visits all his host,
Bids them good morrow with a modest smile
And calls them brothers, friends, and countrymen.
Upon his royal face there is no note   35
How dread an army hath enrounded him;
Nor doth he dedicate one jot of color
Unto the weary and all-watched night,
But freshly looks, and overbears attaint
With cheerful semblance and sweet majesty;   40
That every wretch, pining and pale before,
Beholding him, plucks comfort from his looks.
A largess universal, like the sun,
His liberal eye doth give to every one,
Thawing cold fear, that mean and gentle all   45
Behold, as may unworthiness define,
A little touch of Harry in the night.
And so our scene must to the battle fly;
Where (O for pity!) we shall much disgrace
With four or five most vile and ragged foils,   50
Right ill-disposed in brawl ridiculous,

53. **Minding:** being reminded of, or seeing in your mind's eye.

▬▬▬▬▬▬▬▬▬▬▬▬▬▬▬▬

[**IV. i.**] All the English realize that their situation is grave and they will be lucky to come through the morrow's battle alive. The King talks with some of his soldiers, who are unaware of his identity, and exchanges gloves with one Williams, whose plain speech has angered him. Each is to challenge the other after the battle when he recognizes his own glove. The attitudes expressed by his men have made the King acutely aware that their fate is his responsibility. He soliloquizes on the heavy burdens of kingship and appeals to God for support.

▬▬▬▬▬▬▬▬▬▬▬▬▬▬

5. **soul:** i.e., heart, basic core.
9. **outward consciences:** that is, in contrast to our own inmost consciences.
11. **dress us fairly:** well prepare ourselves.
16. **churlish:** inhospitable; literally, niggardly.

The name of Agincourt. Yet sit and see,
Minding true things by what their mock'ries be.

Exit.

[Scene I. France. The English camp at Agincourt.]

Enter the *King, Bedford,* and *Gloucester.*

King. Gloucester, 'tis true that we are in great
          danger;
The greater therefore should our courage be.
Good morrow, brother Bedford. God Almighty!
There is some soul of goodness in things evil,   5
Would men observingly distill it out;
For our bad neighbor makes us early stirrers,
Which is both healthful, and good husbandry.
Besides, they are our outward consciences,
And preachers to us all, admonishing   10
That we should dress us fairly for our end.
Thus may we gather honey from the weed
And make a moral of the Devil himself.

Enter *Erpingham.*

Good morrow, old Sir Thomas Erpingham.
A good soft pillow for that good white head   15
Were better than a churlish turf of France.
   Erp. Not so, my liege. This lodging likes me better,
Since I may say "Now lie I like a king."
   King. 'Tis good for men to love their present pains

20. **Upon example:** with the example of another before them.

21. **out of doubt:** without question.

22. **defunct:** synonymous with dead.

24. **With casted slough and fresh legerity:** i.e., revived, like a snake that has cast its old skin and shows new vigor.

26. **Commend me to:** give my dutiful greetings to.

36. **God-a-mercy:** i.e., God have mercy, an expression of thanks.

38. **Qui va là:** who goes there.

43. **Trailst thou the puissant pike:** Pistolese for "Are you a member of the infantry?"

44. **Even:** exactly.

Upon example: so the spirit is eased;　　　　　　20
And when the mind is quick'ned, out of doubt
The organs, though defunct and dead before,
Break up their drowsy grave and newly move
With casted slough and fresh legerity.
Lend me thy cloak, Sir Thomas. Brothers both,　　25
Commend me to the princes in our camp;
Do my good morrow to them, and anon
Desire them all to my pavilion.

　Glouc. We shall, my liege.
　Erp. Shall I attend your Grace?　　　　　　30
　King.　　　　　　　　　　No, my good knight.
Go with my brothers to my lords of England.
I and my bosom must debate awhile,
And then I would no other company.
　Erp. The Lord in heaven bless thee, noble Harry!　35
　　　　　　　　　　Exeunt [all but the King].
　King. God-a-mercy, old heart! thou speakst cheer-
　　fully.

　　　　　　Enter *Pistol.*

　Pist. Qui va là?
　King. A friend.
　Pist. Discuss unto me, art thou officer;　　　40
Or art thou base, common, and popular?
　King. I am a gentleman of a company.
　Pist. Trailst thou the puissant pike?
　King. Even so. What are you?
　Pist. As good a gentleman as the Emperor.　　45
　King. Then you are a better than the King.

48. imp of fame: offspring of a famous house.

59. Saint Davy's day: March 1, the anniversary of the Welsh victory over the Saxons, which Welshmen celebrate by wearing the national symbol, the leek, in their hats.

64. figo: see [III. vi.] 57.

67. sorts: suits.

70. admiration: marvel.

Pist. The King's a bawcock, and a heart of gold,
A lad of life, an imp of fame,
Of parents good, of fist most valiant.
I kiss his dirty shoe, and from heartstring   50
I love the lovely bully. What is thy name?

King. Harry le Roy.

Pist. Le Roy? A Cornish name. Art thou of Cornish
   crew?

King. No, I am a Welshman.   55

Pist. Knowst thou Fluellen?

King. Yes.

Pist. Tell him I'll knock his leek about his pate
Upon Saint Davy's day.

King. Do not you wear your dagger in your cap   60
that day, lest he knock that about yours.

Pist. Art thou his friend?

King. And his kinsman too.

Pist. The figo for thee then!

King. I thank you. God be with you!   65

Pist. My name is Pistol called.   *Exit. Manet King.*

King. It sorts well with your fierceness.

Enter *Fluellen* and *Gower.*

Gow. Captain Fluellen!

Flu. Sol in the name of Jesu Christ, speak fewer. It
is the greatest admiration in the universal world,   70
when the true and aunchient prerogatifes and laws of
the wars is not kept. If you would take the pains but
to examine the wars of Pompey the Great, you shall
find, I warrant you, that there is no tiddle taddle nor

78. modesty: moderation; see **modest,** [II. iv.] 37.

pibble pabble in Pompey's camp. I warrant you, you 75
shall find the ceremonies of the wars, and the cares of
it, and the forms of it, and the sobriety of it, and the
modesty of it, to be otherwise.

Gow. Why, the enemy is loud; you hear him all
night.   80

Flu. If the enemy is an ass and a fool and a prating
coxcomb, is it meet, think you, that we should also,
look you, be an ass and a fool and a prating coxcomb?
In your own conscience now?

Gow. I will speak lower.   85

Flu. I pray you and beseech you that you will.
                    Exeunt [*Gower and Fluellen*].

King. Though it appear a little out of fashion,
There is much care and valor in this Welshman.

Enter three Soldiers, *John Bates, Alexander Court,*
                and *Michael Williams.*

Court. Brother John Bates, is not that the morning
which breaks yonder?   90

Bates. I think it be; but we have no great cause to
desire the approach of day.

Will. We see yonder the beginning of the day, but
I think we shall never see the end of it. Who goes
there?   95

King. A friend.

Will. Under what captain serve you?

King. Under Sir Thomas Erpingham.

Will. A good old commander and a most kind gentleman. I pray you, what thinks he of our estate?   100

106-7. **element:** heavens.

111. **stoop:** i.e., swoop down like a hawk to its prey.

113. **relish:** taste; i.e., they are similar in nature.

114-15. **possess him with any appearance of fear:** show any signs of fear that the King may see.

120. **at all adventures:** no matter what the risk; **quit:** finished.

122. **my conscience:** my heartfelt belief.

King. Even as men wracked upon a sand, that look
to be washed off the next tide.

Bates. He hath not told his thought to the King?

King. No; nor is it not meet he should. For though
I speak it to you, I think the King is but a man, as I   105
am. The violet smells to him as it doth to me; the element shows to him as it doth to me; all his senses
have but human conditions. His ceremonies laid by,
in his nakedness he appears but a man; and though
his affections are higher mounted than ours, yet, when   110
they stoop, they stoop with the like wing. Therefore,
when he sees reason of fears, as we do, his fears, out
of doubt, be of the same relish as ours are. Yet, in
reason, no man should possess him with any appearance of fear, lest he, by showing it, should dishearten   115
his army.

Bates. He may show what outward courage he will;
but I believe, as cold a night as 'tis, he could wish
himself in Thames up to the neck; and so I would he
were, and I by him, at all adventures, so we were quit   120
here.

King. By my troth, I will speak my conscience of
the King: I think he would not wish himself anywhere but where he is.

Bates. Then I would he were here alone. So should   125
he be sure to be ransomed, and a many poor men's
lives saved.

King. I dare say you love him not so ill to wish him
here alone, howsoever you speak this to feel other
men's minds. Methinks I could not die anywhere so   130

145. rawly left: left without any provision for their care.

149-50. were against all proportion of subjection: that is, would violate completely the degree of duty which a subject owes his King.

152. sinfully miscarry: die outside a state of grace.

156-57. irreconciled iniquities: sins unconfessed and unatoned for.

contented as in the King's company, his cause being
just and his quarrel honorable.

Will. That's more than we know.

Bates. Ay, or more than we should seek after; for
we know enough if we know we are the King's sub- 135
jects. If his cause be wrong, our obedience to the King
wipes the crime of it out of us.

Will. But if the cause be not good, the King himself
hath a heavy reckoning to make when all those legs
and arms and heads, chopped off in a battle, shall join 140
together at the latter day and cry all "We died at such
a place!" some swearing, some crying for a surgeon,
some upon their wives left poor behind them, some
upon the debts they owe, some upon their children
rawly left. I am afeard there are few die well that die 145
in a battle; for how can they charitably dispose of
anything when blood is their argument? Now, if these
men do not die well, it will be a black matter for the
King that led them to it; who to disobey were against
all proportion of subjection.   150

King. So, if a son that is by his father sent about
merchandise do sinfully miscarry upon the sea, the
imputation of his wickedness, by your rule, should be
imposed upon his father that sent him; or if a servant,
under his master's command transporting a sum of 155
money, be assailed by robbers and die in many irreconciled iniquities, you may call the business of the
master the author of the servant's damnation. But this
is not so. The King is not bound to answer the particular endings of his soldiers, the father of his son, 160
nor the master of his servant; for they purpose not

167-68. broken seals of perjury: false vows of fidelity.

173. beadle: an official who made arrests and saw to the punishment of criminals.

177-78. unprovided: unprepared; lacking the last rites of the church.

180. visited: punished.

187-88. making God so free an offer: i.e., having submitted himself to God's mercy.

their death when they purpose their services. Besides,
there is no king, be his cause never so spotless, if it
come to the arbitrement of swords, can try it out with
all unspotted soldiers. Some (peradventure) have on 165
them the guilt of premeditated and contrived murder;
some, of beguiling virgins with the broken seals of
perjury; some, making the wars their bulwark, that
have before gored the gentle bosom of peace with
pillage and robbery. Now, if these men have defeated 170
the law and outrun native punishment, though they
can outstrip men, they have no wings to fly from God.
War is his beadle, war is his vengeance; so that here
men are punished for before-breach of the King's laws
in now the King's quarrel. Where they feared the 175
death, they have borne life away; and where they
would be safe, they perish. Then if they die unprovided, no more is the King guilty of their damnation
than he was before guilty of those impieties for the
which they are now visited. Every subject's duty is 180
the King's, but every subject's soul is his own. Therefore should every soldier in the wars do as every sick
man in his bed—wash every mote out of his conscience; and dying so, death is to him advantage; or
not dying, the time was blessedly lost wherein such 185
preparation was gained; and in him that escapes, it
were not sin to think that, making God so free an
offer, he let him outlive that day to see his greatness
and to teach others how they should prepare.

Will. 'Tis certain, every man that dies ill, the ill 190
upon his own head—the King is not to answer it.

201. **pay**: punish.
202. **elder-gun**: that is, a popgun made of elder wood.
207. **something too round**: somewhat too blunt.
213. **gage**: token.

Bates. I do not desire he should answer for me, and yet I determine to fight lustily for him.

King. I myself heard the King say he would not be ransomed.   195

Will. Ay, he said so, to make us fight cheerfully; but when our throats are cut, he may be ransomed, and we ne'er the wiser.

King. If I live to see it, I will never trust his word after.   200

Will. You pay him then! That's a perilous shot out of an elder-gun that a poor and a private displeasure can do against a monarch! You may as well go about to turn the sun to ice with fanning in his face with a peacock's feather. You'll never trust his word after!   205 Come, 'tis a foolish saying.

King. Your reproof is something too round. I should be angry with you if the time were convenient.

Will. Let it be a quarrel between us if you live.   210

King. I embrace it.

Will. How shall I know thee again?

King. Give me any gage of thine, and I will wear it in my bonnet. Then, if ever thou darest acknowledge it, I will make it my quarrel.   215

Will. Here's my glove. Give me another of thine.

King. There.

Will. This will I also wear in my cap. If ever thou come to me and say, after tomorrow, "This is my glove," by this hand, I will take thee a box on the ear.   220

King. If ever I live to see it, I will challenge it.

Will. Thou darest as well be hanged.

230, 232. **crowns:** a pun on coins and heads.

233. **a clipper:** one who mutilated currency by chipping bits of gold from it; an offense which was treason according to English law.

235. **careful:** the literal meaning: full of care.

238-40. **subject to the breath/ Of every fool:** exposed as the topic of conversation of even the least of his subjects; **whose sense no more can feel/ But his own wringing:** who is sensitive only to his own personal afflictions.

247. **comings-in:** income.

249. **What is thy soul of adoration:** what is the real value of reverence of you.

King. Well, I will do it, though I take thee in the
King's company.

Will. Keep thy word. Fare thee well.   225

Bates. Be friends, you English fools, be friends!
We have French quarrels enow, if you could tell
how to reckon.

King. Indeed the French may lay twenty French
crowns to one they will beat us, for they bear them   230
on their shoulders; but it is no English treason to cut
French crowns, and tomorrow the King himself will
be a clipper.

                                Exeunt Soldiers.

Upon the King! Let us our lives, our souls,
Our debts, our careful wives,   235
Our children, and our sins, lay on the King!
We must bear all. O hard condition,
Twin-born with greatness, subject to the breath
Of every fool, whose sense no more can feel
But his own wringing! What infinite heart's-ease   240
Must kings neglect that private men enjoy!
And what have kings that privates have not too,
Save ceremony, save general ceremony?
And what art thou, thou idol Ceremony?
What kind of god art thou, that sufferst more   245
Of mortal griefs than do thy worshipers?
What are thy rents? What are thy comings-in?
O Ceremony, show me but thy worth!
What is thy soul of adoration?
Art thou aught else but place, degree, and form,   250
Creating awe and fear in other men?
Wherein thou art less happy being feared

258. **With titles blown from adulation:** i.e., do you think the breath of flattery can cool your fever by blowing upon it. **Blown** is used in two senses, the second being that of "swelled," "inflated."

259. **flexure:** bowing.

263. **find:** expose.

267. **farced:** literally, stuffed; unnaturally puffed out.

274. **distressful bread:** bread painfully earned.

279. **Hyperion:** another name for the sun god.

Than they in fearing.
What drinkst thou oft, instead of homage sweet,
But poisoned flattery? O, be sick, great greatness,   255
And bid thy ceremony give thee cure!
Thinkst thou the fiery fever will go out
With titles blown from adulation?
Will it give place to flexure and low bending?
Canst thou, when thou commandst the beggar's knee, 260
Command the health of it? No, thou proud dream,
That playst so subtly with a king's repose.
I am a king that find thee; and I know
'Tis not the balm, the scepter, and the ball,
The sword, the mace, the crown imperial,   265
The intertissued robe of gold and pearl,
The farced title running fore the king,
The throne he sits on, nor the tide of pomp
That beats upon the high shore of this world—
No, not all these, thrice-gorgeous ceremony,   270
Not all these, laid in bed majestical,
Can sleep so soundly as the wretched slave,
Who, with a body filled, and vacant mind,
Gets him to rest, crammed with distressful bread;
Never sees horrid night, the child of hell;   275
But like a lackey, from the rise to set,
Sweats in the eye of Phoebus, and all night
Sleeps in Elysium; next day after dawn,
Doth rise and help Hyperion to his horse;
And follows so the ever-running year   280
With profitable labor to his grave;
And but for ceremony, such a wretch,
Winding up days with toil and nights with sleep,

286. **wots:** knows.

288. **Whose hours the peasant best advantages:** that is, the watchful hours of the King profit the peasant more than himself. **Advantages** means benefits.

289. **jealous of:** anxious because of.

299-300. **the fault/ My father made in compassing the crown:** i.e., treason against Richard II in deposing him and assuming the crown, and also possible responsibility for the death of Richard, which Henry IV was believed to have ordered. **Compassing** means achieving.

308. **still:** continually; see [III. vii.] 99.

Had the forehand and vantage of a king.
The slave, a member of the country's peace, 285
Enjoys it; but in gross brain little wots
What watch the king keeps to maintain the peace,
Whose hours the peasant best advantages.

Enter Erpingham.

Erp. My lord, your nobles, jealous of your absence,
Seek through your camp to find you. 290
    King.   Good old knight,
Collect them all together at my tent.
I'll be before thee.
    Erp.   I shall do't, my lord.   _Exit._
    King. O God of battles, steel my soldiers' hearts, 295
Possess them not with fear! Take from them now
The sense of reck'ning, if the opposed numbers
Pluck their hearts from them. Not today, O Lord,
O, not today, think not upon the fault
My father made in compassing the crown! 300
I Richard's body have interred new;
And on it have bestowed more contrite tears
Than from it issued forced drops of blood.
Five hundred poor I have in yearly pay,
Who twice a day their withered hands hold up 305
Toward heaven, to pardon blood; and I have built
Two chantries, where the sad and solemn priests
Sing still for Richard's soul. More will I do,
Though all that I can do is nothing worth,
Since that my penitence comes after all, 310
Imploring pardon.

315. **stay for:** await.

<hr/>

[IV. ii.] In the French camp the Dauphin and some of his noble companions are arming and mounting themselves for the fight. Knowing the state of Henry's forces, they are confident of an overwhelming victory.

<hr/>

2. **Montez à cheval:** to horse; **Varlet, laquais:** valet, lackey.

5. **Via! les eaux et la terre:** literally, "On! the waters and the earth." The Dauphin exhorts his horse to show his mettle: "Onward over water and earth!"

6. **Rien puis? L'air et le feu:** Nothing more? Surely air and fire as well.

7. **Ciel:** heaven.

9-10. **for present service neigh:** i.e., they are impatient for immediate action.

Enter *Gloucester*.

Glouc. My liege!
King. My brother Gloucester's voice. Ay.
I know thy errand; I will go with thee.
The day, my friends, and all things stay for me.   315
                                        Exeunt.

[Scene II. The French camp.]

Enter the *Dauphin, Orleans, Rambures,*
and *Beaumont*.

Orl. The sun doth gild our armor. Up, my lords!
Dau. Montez à cheval! My horse! Varlet, laquais!
  Ha!
Orl. O brave spirit!
Dau. Vial les eaux et la terre—
Orl. Rien puis? L'air et le feu.
Dau. Ciel! cousin Orleans.   5

Enter *Constable*.

Now, my Lord Constable?
Con. Hark how our steeds for present service
  neigh!   10
Dau. Mount them and make incision in their hides,
That their hot blood may spin in English eyes

Single combat.
From Olaus Magnus, *Historia de gentibus septentrionalibus* (1555).

13. **dout:** extinguish.

17. **embattailed:** arrayed for battle.

26. **curtal ax:** cutlass.

28. **sheathe for lack of sport:** i.e., sheathe only for lack of further occasion to use them; see sheathed their swords for lack of argument, [III. i.] 22.

31. **'Tis positive 'gainst all exceptions:** there is no question about it.

35. **hilding:** worthless.

And dout them with superfluous courage, ha!
  Ram. What, will you have them weep our horses'
    blood?   15
How shall we then behold their natural tears?

Enter *Messenger.*

  Mess. The English are embattailed, you French
    peers.
  Con. To horse, you gallant princes! straight to
    horse!   20
Do but behold yond poor and starved band,
And your fair show shall suck away their souls,
Leaving them but the shales and husks of men.
There is not work enough for all our hands,
Scarce blood enough in all their sickly veins   25
To give each naked curtal ax a stain
That our French gallants shall today draw out
And sheathe for lack of sport. Let us but blow on
    them,
The vapor of our valor will o'erturn them.   30
'Tis positive 'gainst all exceptions, lords,
That our superfluous lackeys and our peasants,
Who in unnecessary action swarm
About our squares of battle, were enow
To purge this field of such a hilding foe,   35
Though we upon this mountain's basis by
Took stand for idle speculation,
But that our honors must not. What's to say?
A very little little let us do,

41. **tucket sonance:** sound of the tucket—a call to the cavalry.

42. **dare the field:** daunt the enemy force; a metaphor from hawking. The enemy troops are pictured as paralyzed with fright.

46. **desperate of their bones:** i.e., desperate to save their bones—all that is left of their carcasses.

49. **passing:** exceedingly.

50. **Big Mars seems bankrout in their beggared host:** that is, their impoverished numbers have little appearance of martial worth. **Bankrout** means bankrupt.

51. **beaver:** visor.

54. **Lob:** droop.

56. **gimmaled bit:** a double bit, hinged together.

58. **their executors:** the handlers of their last remains.

60. **suit itself:** clothe itself adequately.

And all is done. Then let the trumpets sound   40
The tucket sonance and the note to mount;
For our approach shall so much dare the field
That England shall couch down in fear and yield.

Enter Grandpré.

  Grand. Why do you stay so long, my lords of
    France?   45
Yond island carrions, desperate of their bones,
Ill-favoredly become the morning field.
Their ragged curtains poorly are let loose,
And our air shakes them passing scornfully.
Big Mars seems bankrout in their beggared host   50
And faintly through a rusty beaver peeps.
The horsemen sit like fixed candlesticks
With torch staves in their hand; and their poor jades
Lob down their heads, dropping the hides and hips,
The gum down roping from their pale-dead eyes,   55
And in their pale dull mouths the gimmaled bit
Lies foul with chawed grass, still and motionless;
And their executors, the knavish crows,
Fly o'er them, all impatient for their hour.
Description cannot suit itself in words   60
To demonstrate the life of such a battle
In life so lifeless as it shows itself.
  Con. They have said their prayers, and they stay
    for death.
  Dau. Shall we go send them dinners and fresh suits   65
And give their fasting horses provender,
And after fight with them?

68. guidon: banner.

[**IV. iii.**] King Henry's nobles consider their odds and note how heavily they are outnumbered. The King, however, cheers them by pointing out that the fewer men in their number the greater will be their honor, and promises that the day of this battle, St. Crispin's Day, will be long remembered in England. The French Herald comes once again to ask whether the King will name a ransom but is denied and sent away. With York leading the foremost troops, the English then move into battle.

7. charge: battle station.

Mars, god of war.
From Vincenzo Cartari, *Imagini de gli dei delli antichi* (1615).

82

Con. I stay but for my guidon. To the field!
I will the banner from a trumpet take
And use it for my haste. Come, come away!   70
The sun is high, and we outwear the day.

                                        Exeunt.

[Scene III. The English camp.]

Enter *Gloucester, Bedford, Exeter, Erpingham* with
    all his host, *Salisbury*, and *Westmoreland*.

Glouc. Where is the King?
Bed. The King himself is rode to view their battle.
West. Of fighting men they have full three-score
    thousand.
Exe. There's five to one; besides, they all are fresh.   5
Sal. God's arm strike with us! 'Tis a fearful odds.
God be wi' you, princes all; I'll to my charge.
If we no more meet till we meet in heaven,
Then joyfully, my noble Lord of Bedford,
My dear Lord Gloucester, and my good Lord Exeter,   10
And my kind kinsman, warriors all, adieu!
Bed. Farewell, good Salisbury, and good luck go
    with thee!
Exe. Farewell, kind lord. Fight valiantly today;
And yet I do thee wrong to mind thee of it,   15
For thou art framed of the firm truth of valor.
                                [*Exit Salisbury.*]
Bed. He is as full of valor as of kindness,
Princely in both.

24-5. we are enow/ To do our country loss: we are enough loss for our country.

30. It yearns me not: it doesn't bother me.

43. fears his fellowship to die with us: is afraid of being my companion in death.

44. Feast of Crispian: the birthday of St. Crispin, patron saint of shoemakers.

Enter the *King*.

West.   O that we now had here
But one ten thousand of those men in England   20
That do no work today!
   King.   What's he that wishes so?
My cousin Westmoreland? No, my fair cousin.
If we are marked to die, we are enow
To do our country loss; and if to live,   25
The fewer men, the greater share of honor.
God's will! I pray thee wish not one man more.
By Jove, I am not covetous for gold,
Nor care I who doth feed upon my cost;
It yearns me not if men my garments wear;   30
Such outward things dwell not in my desires:
But if it be a sin to covet honor,
I am the most offending soul alive.
No, faith, my coz, wish not a man from England.
God's peace! I would not lose so great an honor   35
As one man more methinks would share from me
For the best hope I have. O, do not wish one more!
Rather proclaim it, Westmoreland, through my host,
That he which hath no stomach to this fight,
Let him depart; his passport shall be made,   40
And crowns for convoy put into his purse.
We would not die in that man's company
That fears his fellowship to die with us.
This day is called the Feast of Crispian.
He that outlives this day, and comes safe home,   45
Will stand a-tiptoe when this day is named

47. **rouse him:** straighten himself up with pride.
54. **with advantages:** i.e., with additional colorful details that may not be true.

And rouse him at the name of Crispian.
He that shall live this day, and see old age,
Will yearly on the vigil feast his neighbors
And say "Tomorrow is Saint Crispian."   50
Then will he strip his sleeve and show his scars,
And say "These wounds I had on Crispin's day."
Old men forget; yet all shall be forgot,
But he'll remember, with advantages,
What feats he did that day. Then shall our names,   55
Familiar in his mouth as household words—
Harry the King, Bedford and Exeter,
Warwick and Talbot, Salisbury and Gloucester—
Be in their flowing cups freshly rememb'red.
This story shall the good man teach his son;   60
And Crispin Crispian shall ne'er go by,
From this day to the ending of the world,
But we in it shall be remembered—
We few, we happy few, we band of brothers;
For he today that sheds his blood with me   65
Shall be my brother. Be he ne'er so vile,
This day shall gentle his condition;
And gentlemen in England now abed
Shall think themselves accursed they were not here,
And hold their manhoods cheap whiles any speaks   70
That fought with us upon Saint Crispin's day.

                    Enter *Salisbury*.

  Sal. My sovereign lord, bestow yourself with
    speed.
The French are bravely in their battles set

75. **expedience:** expedition, speed.
89. **compound:** reach agreement.
102. **achieve:** conquer; see [III. iii.] 8 and [III. v.] 64.

And will with all expedience charge on us.   75
  King. All things are ready, if our minds be so.
  West. Perish the man whose mind is backward
    now!
  King. Thou dost not wish more help from England,
    coz?   80
  West. God's will, my liege! would you and I alone,
Without more help, could fight this royal battle!
  King. Why, now thou hast unwished five thousand
    men!
Which likes me better than to wish us one.   85
You know your places. God be with you all!

Tucket. Enter *Montjoy.*

  Mont. Once more I come to know of thee, King
    Harry,
If for thy ransom thou wilt now compound,
Before thy most assured overthrow;   90
For certainly thou art so near the gulf
Thou needs must be englutted. Besides, in mercy,
The Constable desires thee thou wilt mind
Thy followers of repentance, that their souls
May make a peaceful and a sweet retire   95
From off these fields, where (wretches!) their poor
    bodies
Must lie and fester.
  King.   Who hath sent thee now?
  Mont. The Constable of France.   100
  King. I pray thee bear my former answer back:
Bid them achieve me, and then sell my bones.

117-19. like to the bullet's grazing,/ Break out into a second course of mischief,/ Killing in relapse of mortality: like a bullet which ricochets to inflict a mortal wound, the dead soldiers may kill indirectly by the pestilence breeding in their corpses.

129-31. They'll be in fresher robes, or they will pluck/ The gay new coats o'er the French soldiers' heads/ And turn them out of service: they will have fresher clothes if they have to strip the French soldiers of their raiment and dismiss them—to their deaths. The phrase **turn them out of service** speaks of the French as though they were servants.

Good God! why should they mock poor fellows thus?
The man that once did sell the lion's skin
While the beast lived, was killed with hunting him.   105
A many of our bodies shall no doubt
Find native graves; upon the which, I trust,
Shall witness live in brass of this day's work;
And those that leave their valiant bones in France,
Dying like men, though buried in your dunghills,   110
They shall be famed; for there the sun shall greet
          them
And draw their honors reeking up to heaven,
Leaving their earthly parts to choke your clime,
The smell whereof shall breed a plague in France.   115
Mark then abounding valor in our English,
That, being dead, like to the bullet's grazing,
Break out into a second course of mischief,
Killing in relapse of mortality.
Let me speak proudly. Tell the Constable   120
We are but warriors for the working day.
Our gayness and our gilt are all besmirched
With rainy marching in the painful field.
There's not a piece of feather in our host—
Good argument, I hope, we will not fly—   125
And time hath worn us into slovenry.
But, by the mass, our hearts are in the trim;
And my poor soldiers tell me, yet ere night
They'll be in fresher robes, or they will pluck
The gay new coats o'er the French soldiers' heads   130
And turn them out of service. If they do this
(As, if God please, they shall), my ransom then
Will soon be levied. Herald, save thou thy labor.

143. **vaward:** vanguard; the foremost line of attack.

[IV. iv.] Pistol and the boy, his remaining companion, have captured a French soldier. With the boy interpreting for him, Pistol, whose French is inadequate, arranges to free the soldier instead of killing him, for a ransom of two hundred crowns. The boy expresses his disgust at his service with Pistol before he goes to join the lackeys who guard the luggage.

2-3. **Je pense que vous êtes le gentilhomme de bonne qualité:** I believe that you are a gentleman of quality.

4. **Callino custore me:** a contemporary Irish song contained a similar phrase and Pistol may be echoing that.

6. **Seigneur Dieu:** Lord God.

Come thou no more for ransom, gentle herald.
They shall have none, I swear, but these my joints; 135
Which if they have as I will leave 'em them,
Shall yield them little, tell the Constable.
    Mont. I shall, King Harry. And so fare thee well.
Thou never shalt hear herald any more.   *Exit.*
    King. I fear thou wilt once more come again for 140
    ransom.

Enter York.

    York. My lord, most humbly on my knee I beg
The leading of the vaward.
    King. Take it, brave York. Now, soldiers, march
    away;   145
And how thou pleasest, God, dispose the day!
        Exeunt.

[Scene IV. The field of battle.]

*Alarum. Excursions. Enter Pistol, French Soldier,
Boy.*

    Pist. Yield, cur!
    French. Je pense que vous êtes le gentilhomme de
bonne qualité.
    Pist. Quality! Callino custore me! Art thou a gentle-
man? What is thy name? Discuss.   5
    French. O Seigneur Dieu!

7. **Signieur Dew should be a gentleman:** Pistol apparently understands **Signieur** to mean Lord, so he concludes that his captor must be a gentleman.

8. **Perpend:** consider.

9. **fox:** i.e., sword, the name deriving from the trade-mark of a certain type of sword of good quality.

11. **Egregious:** extraordinary; see [II. i.] 46.

12. **prenez miséricorde! ayez pitié de moi:** take mercy! have pity on me.

13. **Moy:** misinterpreted by Pistol as meaning a coin.

14. **rim:** belly.

16-7. **Est-il impossible d'échapper la force de ton bras:** is it impossible to escape the force of his arm.

28. **firk:** beat.

29. **ferret:** worry, as a ferret does a rat.

34-6. **Il me commande à vous dire que vous faites vous prêt; car ce soldat ici est disposé tout à cette heure de couper votre gorge:** he commands me to say to you that you should prepare yourself; for this soldier is disposed immediately to cut your throat.

Pist. O Signieur Dew should be a gentleman.
Perpend my words, O Signieur Dew, and mark.
O Signieur Dew, thou diest on point of fox,
Except, O signieur, thou do give to me   10
Egregious ransom.

   French. O, prenez miséricorde! ayez pitié de moi!

   Pist. Moy shall not serve. I will have forty moys;
Or I will fetch thy rim out at thy throat
In drops of crimson blood.   15

   French. Est-il impossible d'échapper la force de
ton bras?

   Pist. Brass, cur?
Thou damned and luxurious mountain goat,
Offerst me brass?   20

   French. O, pardonnez-moi!

   Pist. Sayst thou me so? Is that a ton of moys?
Come hither, boy; ask me this slave in French
What is his name.

   Boy. Écoutez. Comment êtes-vous appelé?   25

   French. Monsieur le Fer.

   Boy. He says his name is Master Fer.

   Pist. Master Fer? I'll fer him, and firk him, and
ferret him! Discuss the same in French unto him.

   Boy. I do not know the French for "fer," and   30
"ferret," and "firk."

   Pist. Bid him prepare, for I will cut his throat.

   French. Que dit-il, monsieur?

   Boy. Il me commande à vous dire que vous faites
vous prêt; car ce soldat ici est disposé tout à cette   35
heure de couper votre gorge.

37. **Owy, cuppele gorge, permafoy:** Pistol's phonetic French: O, yes, cut the throat, on my honor.

49. **Petit monsieur, que dit-il:** little master, what did he say.

50-3. **Encore . . . franchisement:** even though it is against his judgment to pardon any prisoner, nevertheless, for the crowns that you have promised him, he is glad to give you liberty.

54-7. **Sur . . . d'Angleterre:** the boy renders a free translation of the passage in ll. 59-63.

66. **Suivez-vous le grand Capitaine:** follow the great captain.

Pist. Owy, cuppele gorge, permafoy!
Peasant, unless thou give me crowns, brave crowns;
Or mangled shalt thou be by this my sword.

French. O, je vous supplie, pour l'amour de Dieu,   40
me pardonner! Je suis gentilhomme de bonne maison.
Gardez ma vie, et je vous donnerai deux cents écus.

Pist. What are his words?

Boy. He prays you to save his life. He is a gentleman of a good house, and for his ransom he will give   45
you two hundred crowns.

Pist. Tell him my fury shall abate, and I
The crowns will take.

French. Petit monsieur, que dit-il?

Boy. Encore qu'il est contre son jurement de par-   50
donner aucun prisonnier, néanmoins, pour les écus
que vous l'avez promis, il est content de vous donner la liberté, le franchisement.

French. Sur mes genoux je vous donne mille re-
mercîments; et je m'estime heureux que je suis tombé   55
entre les mains d'un chevalier, je pense, le plus brave,
vaillant, et très-distingué seigneur d'Angleterre.

Pist. Expound unto me, boy.

Boy. He gives you, upon his knees, a thousand
thanks; and he esteems himself happy that he hath   60
fall'n into the hands of one (as he thinks) the most
brave, valorous, and thrice-worthy signieur of England.

Pist. As I suck blood, I will some mercy show!
Follow me, cur.   [*Exit.*]   65

Boy. Suivez-vous le grand Capitaine.

                              [*Exit French Soldier.*]

70-1. **roaring devil i' the old play**: in the old morality plays the devil was a comic character.

[IV. v.] The French forces have been forced to turn and fly; the Dauphin and the other French lords lament the loss of the shining victory they had foreseen.

1. **diable**: the devil.
2. **Seigneur! le jour est perdu, tout est perdu**: Lord! the day is lost, all is lost.
3. **confounded**: destroyed, lost; see [III. i.] 14.
6. **méchante fortune**: evil fortune.
8. **perdurable**: enduring.

I did never know so full a voice issue from so empty
a heart; but the saying is true, "The empty vessel
makes the greatest sound." Bardolph and Nym had
ten times more valor than this roaring devil i' the old   70
play that every one may pare his nails with a wooden
dagger; and they are both hanged; and so would this
be, if he durst steal anything adventurously. I must
stay with the lackeys with the luggage of our camp.
The French might have a good prey of us, if he knew   75
of it; for there is none to guard it but boys.

                                        [*Exit.*]

[Scene V. Another part of the field of battle.]

Enter *Constable, Orleans, Bourbon, Dauphin,* and
                Rambures.

    Con. O diable!
    Orl. O Seigneur! le jour est perdu, tout est perdu!
    Dau. Mort de ma vie! all is confounded, all!
Reproach and everlasting shame
Sits mocking in our plumes.   5

                          A short alarum.
O méchante fortune! Do not run away.
    Con. Why, all our ranks are broke.
    Dau. O perdurable shame! Let's stab ourselves.
Be these the wretches that we played at dice for?
    Orl. Is this the king we sent to for his ransom?   10

20. **on heaps:** in a body.

[IV. vi.] As King Henry and Exeter are contemplating the outcome of the battle with some satisfaction, though both are grieved at the deaths of Suffolk and York, the newly heartened French begin a fresh assault. The King orders every English soldier to kill his prisoners.

Battle scene.
From Olaus Magnus, *Historia de gentibus septentrionalibus* (1555).

Bour. Shame, and eternal shame! nothing but
    shame!
Let's die in honor. Once more back again!
And he that will not follow Bourbon now,
Let him go hence, and with his cap in hand   15
Like a base pander hold the chamber door
Whilst by a slave, no gentler than my dog,
His fairest daughter is contaminated.
    Con. Disorder, that hath spoiled us, friend us now!
Let us on heaps go offer up our lives.   20
    Orl. We are enow yet living in the field
To smother up the English in our throngs,
If any order might be thought upon.
    Bour. The devil take order now! I'll to the throng.
Let life be short; else shame will be too long.   25

                         Exeunt.

[Scene VI. Another part of the field.]

Alarum. Enter the *King* and his *Train,* [*Exeter,* and
    others,] with *Prisoners.*

    King. Well have we done, thrice-valiant country-
    men;
But all's not done, yet keep the French the field.
    Exe. The Duke of York commends him to your
    Majesty.   5
    King. Lives he, good uncle? Thrice within this hour
I saw him down; thrice up again and fighting.
From helmet to the spur all blood he was.

10. **Larding:** fattening, enriching.

11. **honor-owing:** i.e., possessing honor; honorable.

13. **haggled:** hacked.

23. **raught:** reached.

25. **Commend my service:** not "praise what I have done," but "tender my loyal duty"; see [IV. i.] 26.

33. **all my mother:** all of the womanly softness in my nature.

36-7. **perforce:** against my will; **compound/ With:** make my peace with, come to terms with; see [IV. iii.] 89.

37. **issue:** give forth (tears).

Exe. In which array, brave soldier, doth he lie,
Larding the plain; and by his bloody side,   10
Yoke-fellow to his honor-owing wounds,
The noble Earl of Suffolk also lies.
Suffolk first died; and York, all haggled over,
Comes to him, where in gore he lay insteeped,
And takes him by the beard, kisses the gashes   15
That bloodily did yawn upon his face,
And cries aloud, "Tarry, dear cousin Suffolk!
My soul shall thine keep company to heaven.
Tarry, sweet soul, for mine, then fly abreast;
As in this glorious and well-foughten field   20
We kept together in our chivalry!"
Upon these words I came and cheered him up.
He smiled me in the face, raught me his hand,
And, with a feeble gripe, says "Dear my lord,
Commend my service to my sovereign."   25
So did he turn, and over Suffolk's neck
He threw his wounded arm and kissed his lips;
And so, espoused to death, with blood he sealed
A testament of noble-ending love.
The pretty and sweet manner of it forced   30
Those waters from me which I would have stopped;
But I had not so much of man in me,
And all my mother came into mine eyes
And gave me up to tears.
    King.   I blame you not;   35
For, hearing this, I must perforce compound
With mistful eyes, or they will issue too.

                                            Alarum.
But hark! what new alarum is this same?

[IV. vii.] The French, in order to gain some measure of victory, have despoiled the luggage of the English forces and killed the boys who were guarding it. Montjoy comes again, but this time has no hope of arranging the King's ransom; he only asks on behalf of the French that they be allowed to gather their dead for burial. He concedes an English victory. Henry inquires the name of a nearby castle and is told that it is known as Agincourt.

Among his men on the field the King notes Williams wearing his own glove in his cap and questions him about the gage. He then asks Fluellen to wear the other glove and tells him that it came from the Duke d'Alençon. Henry plans a comic encounter between Fluellen and Williams.

2. **arrant:** absolute; see [III. vi.] 62.
16-7. **magnanimous:** great in soul.

The French have reinforced their scattered men.
Then every soldier kill his prisoners!   40
Give the word through.

                                        Exeunt.

[Scene VII. Another part of the field.]

Enter *Fluellen* and *Gower*.

Flu. Kill the poys and the luggage? 'Tis expressly
against the law of arms. 'Tis as arrant a piece of
knavery, mark you now, as can be offert. In your conscience, now, is it not?

Gow. 'Tis certain there's not a boy left alive; and   5
the cowardly rascals that ran from the battle ha' done
this slaughter. Besides, they have burned and carried
away all that was in the King's tent; wherefore the
King most worthily hath caused every soldier to cut
his prisoner's throat. O, 'tis a gallant king!   10

Flu. Ay, he was porn at Monmouth, Captain
Gower. What call you the town's name where
Alexander the Pig was born?

Gow. Alexander the Great.

Flu. Why, I pray you, is not "pig" great? The pig, 15
or the great, or the mighty, or the huge, or the magnanimous are all one reckonings, save the phrase is a
little variations.

Gow. I think Alexander the Great was born in

33. **figures:** parallels.
47. **great belly doublet:** the male upper garment called the doublet was often stuffed with hair or fabric, and the peasecod belly doublet, fashionable during part of the period, was stuffed in a downward curve so that it overhung the waistline in somewhat of a point. Fluellen probably refers to Falstaff's natural girth, however.

Macedon. His father was called Philip of Macedon, 20
as I take it.

Flu. I think it is in Macedon where Alexander is
porn. I tell you, Captain, if you look in the maps of
the 'orld, I warrant you sall find, in the comparisons
between Macedon and Monmouth, that the situations, 25
look you, is both alike. There is a river in Macedon,
and there is also moreover a river at Monmouth. It is
called Wye at Monmouth; but it is out of my prains
what is the name of the other river. But 'tis all one;
'tis alike as my fingers is to my fingers, and there is 30
salmons in both. If you mark Alexander's life well,
Harry of Monmouth's life is come after it indifferent
well; for there is figures in all things. Alexander, God
knows and you know, in his rages, and his furies, and
his wraths, and his cholers, and his moods, and his 35
displeasures, and his indignations, and also being a
little intoxicates in his prains, did, in his ales and his
angers, look you, kill his best friend, Cleitus.

Gow. Our King is not like him in that. He never
killed any of his friends. 40

Flu. It is not well done, mark you now, to take the
tales out of my mouth ere it is made and finished. I
speak but in the figures and comparisons of it. As
Alexander killed his friend Cleitus, being in his ales
and his cups, so also Harry Monmouth, being in his 45
right wits and his good judgments, turned away the
fat knight with the great belly doublet. He was full
of jests, and gipes, and knaveries, and mocks. I have
forgot his name.

Gow. Sir John Falstaff. 50

60. **skirr:** scurry.

70. **fined:** staked, probably with the second meaning "refined," since he has offered his bones in place of gold coins.

Flu. That is he. I'll tell you there is good men porn at Monmouth.

Gow. Here comes his Majesty.

Alarum. Enter KING HARRY, [*Warwick, Gloucester, Exeter,* and others,] with *Prisoners. Flourish.*

King. I was not angry since I came to France
Until this instant. Take a trumpet, herald;   55
Ride thou unto the horsemen on yond hill.
If they will fight with us, bid them come down,
Or void the field. They do offend our sight.
If they'll do neither, we will come to them
And make them skirr away as swift as stones   60
Enforced from the old Assyrian slings.
Besides, we'll cut the throats of those we have;
And not a man of them that we shall take
Shall taste our mercy. Go and tell them so.

Enter MONTJOY [*the Herald*].

Exe. Here comes the herald of the French, my   65
    liege.
Glouc. His eyes are humbler than they used to be.
King. How now? What means this, herald? Knowst
    thou not
That I have fined these bones of mine for ransom?   70
Comest thou again for ransom?
    Herald.   No, great King.

75. book: list.

77. woe the while: alas that one should see such a day.

78. mercenary blood: the blood of ordinary soldiers, who fought for pay rather than for honor, as the nobles did.

82. Yerk: kick.

88. peer: appear.

92. hard: near.

I come to thee for charitable license
That we may wander o'er this bloody field
To book our dead, and then to bury them;   75
To sort our nobles from our common men;
For many of our princes (woe the while!)
Lie drowned and soaked in mercenary blood;
So do our vulgar drench their peasant limbs
In blood of princes; and the wounded steeds   80
Fret fetlock-deep in gore and with wild rage
Yerk out their armed heels at their dead masters,
Killing them twice. O, give us leave, great King,
To view the field in safety and dispose
Of their dead bodies!   85
 King.   I tell thee truly, herald,
I know not if the day be ours or no;
For yet a many of your horsemen peer
And gallop o'er the field.
 Herald.   The day is yours.   90
 King. Praised be God and not our strength for it!
What is this castle called that stands hard by?
 Herald. They call it Agincourt.
 King. Then call we this the field of Agincourt,
Fought on the day of Crispin Crispianus.   95
 Flu. Your grandfather of famous memory, an't
please your Majesty, and your great-uncle Edward
the Plack Prince of Wales, as I have read in the
chronicles, fought a most prave pattle here in France.
 King. They did, Fluellen.   100
 Flu. Your Majesty says very true. If your Majesties
is remm'bred of it, the Welshmen did good service

118. **honest:** honorable.
121. **just notice:** exact reckoning.

in a garden where leeks did grow, wearing leeks in
their Monmouth caps; which your Majesty know to
this hour is an honorable badge of the service; and I   105
do believe your Majesty takes no scorn to wear the
leek upon Saint Tavy's day.

King. I wear it for a memorable honor;
For I am Welsh, you know, good countryman.

Flu. All the water in Wye cannot wash your   110
Majesty's Welsh plood out of your pody, I can tell
you that. God pless it and preserve it, as long as it
pleases his grace, and his majesty too!

King. Thanks, good my countryman.

Flu. By Jeshu, I am your Majesty's countryman, I   115
care not who know it! I will confess it to all the 'orld.
I need not to be ashamed of your Majesty, praised be
God, so long as your Majesty is an honest man.

King. God keep me so!

Enter *Williams.*

                      Our heralds go with him.   120
Bring me just notice of the numbers dead
On both our parts.

            [*Exeunt Heralds with Montjoy.*]
            Call yonder fellow hither.

Exe. Soldier, you must come to the King.

King. Soldier, why wearst thou that glove in thy   125
    cap?

Will. An't please your Majesty, 'tis the gage of one
that I should fight withal, if he be alive.

141. **quite from the answer of his degree:**
quite above the necessity, in honor, of answering
the challenge of one so much beneath him.

142-43. **as good a gentleman as the Devil:**
Shakespeare expresses the same traditional idea in
King Lear, III. iv. 143: "The prince of darkness is
a gentleman!"

145. **perjured:** forsworn.

146. **jack sauce:** impudent fellow.

King. An Englishman?

Will. An't please your Majesty, a rascal that swag- 130
gered with me last night; who, if 'a live and ever dare
to challenge this glove, I have sworn to take him a
box o' the ear; or if I can see my glove in his cap,
which he swore, as he was a soldier, he would wear
(if alive), I will strike it out soundly.   135

King. What think you, Captain Fluellen? Is it fit
this soldier keep his oath?

Flu. He is a craven and a villain else, an't please
your Majesty, in my conscience.

King. It may be his enemy is a gentleman of great 140
sort, quite from the answer of his degree.

Flu. Though he be as good a gentleman as the
Devil is, as Lucifer and Belzebub himself, it is necessary, look your Grace, that he keep his vow and his
oath. If he be perjured, see you now, his reputation 145
is as arrant a villain and a jack sauce as ever his black
shoe trod upon God's ground and his earth, in my
conscience, la!

King. Then keep thy vow, sirrah, when thou meetst
the fellow.   150

Will. So I will, my liege, as I live.

King. Who servest thou under?

Will. Under Captain Gower, my liege.

Flu. Gower is a good captain and is good knowledge and literatured in the wars.   155

King. Call him hither to me, soldier.

Will. I will, my liege.   *Exit.*

King. Here, Fluellen; wear thou this favor for me

178. haply: perhaps; **purchase him:** get for him.

and stick it in thy cap. When Alençon and myself
were down together, I plucked this glove from his 160
helm. If any man challenge this, he is a friend to
Alençon and an enemy to our person. If thou encounter any such, apprehend him, an thou dost me love.

Flu. Your Grace doo's me as great honors as can be
desired in the hearts of his subjects. I would fain see 165
the man, that has but two legs, that shall find himself
aggriefed at this glove, that is all. But I would fain see
it once, and please God of his grace that I might see.

King. Knowst thou Gower?

Flu. He is my dear friend, an please you. 170

King. Pray thee go seek him and bring him to my
tent.

Flu. I will fetch him. *Exit.*

King. My Lord of Warwick, and my brother
Gloucester, 175
Follow Fluellen closely at the heels.
The glove which I have given him for a favor
May haply purchase him a box o' the ear;
It is the soldier's. I by bargain should
Wear it myself. Follow, good cousin Warwick. 180
If that the soldier strike him—as I judge
By his blunt bearing, he will keep his word—
Some sudden mischief may arise of it;
For I do know Fluellen valiant,
And, touched with choler, hot as gunpowder, 185
And quickly will return an injury.
Follow, and see there be no harm between them.
Go you with me, uncle of Exeter.

Exeunt.

[IV. viii.] Williams and Gower come to the King's tent as commanded. Williams immediately notices the glove in Fluellen's cap and strikes him. Fluellen naturally assumes that he is a traitor and is only prevented by Gower from payment in kind when the King enters and reveals the truth of the matter. To make up for the trick he had played upon Williams, he gives him the glove full of money.

An English herald reports ten thousand French dead, all but sixteen hundred being members of the nobility, while the English losses total twenty-nine in all. The King orders his forces to march into the village and humbly to acknowledge the victory as God's. After burying their dead with proper rites they will proceed to Calais to sail for England.

▬▬▬▬▬▬▬▬▬▬▬▬▬▬▬▬▬▬

9. 'Sblood: God's blood.

[Scene VIII. Before King Henry's tent.]

Enter *Gower* and *Williams*.

Will. I warrant it is to knight you, Captain.

Enter *Fluellen*.

Flu. God's will and his pleasure, Captain, I beseech
you now, come apace to the King. There is more good
toward you peradventure than is in your knowledge
to dream of.   5
Will. Sir, know you this glove?
Flu. Know the glove? I know the glove is a glove.
Will. I know this; and thus I challenge it.
                                            Strikes him.
Flu. 'Sblood! an arrant traitor as any's in the uni-
versal world, or in France, or in England!   10
Gow. How now, sir? You villain!
Will. Do you think I'll be forsworn?
Flu. Stand away, Captain Gower. I will give trea-
son his payment into plows, I warrant you.
Will. I am no traitor.   15
Flu. That's a lie in thy throat. I charge you in his
Majesty's name apprehend him. He's a friend of the
Duke Alençon's.

Enter *Warwick* and *Gloucester*.

War. How now, how now? What's the matter?
Flu. My Lord of Warwick, here is (praised be God   20

21. **contagious:** pestilent.

29. **change:** exchange.

33-4. **saving your Majesty's manhood:** an apology for the epithets which follow.

36. **avouchment:** avouch, affirm.

for it!) a most contagious treason come to light, look
you, as you shall desire in a summer's day. Here is his
Majesty.

Enter *King* and *Exeter.*

King. How now? What's the matter?

Flu. My liege, here is a villain and a traitor that,   25
look your Grace, has struck the glove which your
Majesty is take out of the helmet of Alençon.

Will. My liege, this was my glove, here is the fellow of it; and he that I gave it to in change promised
to wear it in his cap. I promised to strike him if he   30
did. I met this man with my glove in his cap, and I
have been as good as my word.

Flu. Your Majesty hear now, saving your Majesty's
manhood, what an arrant, rascally, beggarly, lousy
knave it is! I hope your Majesty is pear me testimony   35
and witness, and will avouchment, that this is the
glove of Alençon that your Majesty is give me, in your
conscience, now.

King. Give me thy glove, soldier. Look, here is the
fellow of it.   40
'Twas I indeed thou promisedst to strike;
And thou hast given me most bitter terms.

Flu. An please your Majesty, let his neck answer
for it, if there is any martial law in the world.

King. How canst thou make me satisfaction?   45

Will. All offenses, my lord, come from the heart.
Never came any from mine that might offend your
Majesty.

Henry the fift.

THis was a King Renowned neere and far,
    A *Mars* of men, a Thunderbolt of war:
At *Agencourt* the French were ouerthrowne,
And *Henry* heyre proclaim'd vnto that Crowne.
In nine yeeres raigne this valiant Prince wan more,
Then all the Kings did after, or before.
Entomb'd at *Westminster* his Carkas lyes,
His foule did (like his Acts) ascend the skyes.

                       Henry

A seventeenth-century eulogy of Henry V.
From John Taylor, *A Memorial of All the English Monarchs*
(1622).

King. It was ourself thou didst abuse.

Will. Your Majesty came not like yourself. You ap-   50
peared to me but as a common man; witness the
night, your garments, your lowliness. And what your
Highness suffered under that shape, I beseech you
take it for your own fault, and not mine; for had you
been as I took you for, I made no offense. Therefore   55
I beseech your Highness pardon me.

King. Here, uncle Exeter, fill this glove with crowns
And give it to this fellow. Keep it, fellow,
And wear it for an honor in thy cap
Till I do challenge it. Give him the crowns;   60
And, Captain, you must needs be friends with him.

Flu. By this day and this light, the fellow has mettle enough in his belly. Hold, there is twelve pence
for you; and I pray you to serve God, and keep you
out of prawls, and prabbles, and quarrels, and dissen-   65
sions, and I warrant you it is the better for you.

Will. I will none of your money.

Flu. It is with a good will. I can tell you it will
serve you to mend your shoes. Come, wherefore
should you be so pashful? Your shoes is not so good.   70
'Tis a good silling, I warrant you, or I will change it.

Enter [an English] *Herald.*

King. Now, herald, are the dead numb'red?
Her. Here is the number of the slaught'red French.
[*Gives a paper.*]
King. What prisoners of good sort are taken, uncle?
Exe. Charles Duke of Orleans, nephew to the King;   75

87. **mercenaries:** common soldiers; see **mercenary**, [IV. vii.] 78.

John Duke of Bourbon and Lord Bouciqualt:
Of other lords and barons, knights and squires,
Full fifteen hundred, besides common men.
    King. This note doth tell me of ten thousand French   80
That in the field lie slain. Of princes, in this number,
And nobles bearing banners, there lie dead
One hundred twenty-six; added to these,
Of knights, esquires, and gallant gentlemen,
Eight thousand and four hundred; of the which,
Five hundred were but yesterday dubbed knights;   85
So that in these ten thousand they have lost
There are but sixteen hundred mercenaries;
The rest are princes, barons, lords, knights, squires,
And gentlemen of blood and quality.
The names of those their nobles that lie dead: 90
Charles Delabreth, High Constable of France;
·Jaques of Chatillon, Admiral of France;
The master of the crossbows, Lord Rambures;
Great Master of France, the brave Sir Guichard
        Dauphin;   95
John Duke of Alençon; Anthony Duke of Brabant,
The brother to the Duke of Burgundy;
And Edward Duke of Bar; of lusty earls,
Grandpré and Roussi, Faulconbridge and Foix,
Beaumont and Marle, Vaudemont and Lestrale.   100
Here was a royal fellowship of death!
Where is the number of our English dead?
                        [*Herald gives another paper.*]
Edward the Duke of York, the Earl of Suffolk,
Sir Richard Ketly, Davy Gam, Esquire;
None else of name; and of all other men   105

A Norwich whiffler.
From Gentleman's Magazine (1852).
(See Cho. V. 13.)

104

But five-and-twenty. O God, thy arm was here!
And not to us, but to thy arm alone,
Ascribe we all! When, without stratagem,
But in plain shock and even play of battle,
Was ever known so great and little loss   110
On one part and on the other? Take it, God,
For it is none but thine!

    Exe.   'Tis wonderful!

    King. Come, go we in procession to the village;
And be it death proclaimed through our host   115
To boast of this, or take that praise from God
Which is his only.

    Flu. Is it not lawful, an please your Majesty, to tell
how many is killed?

    King. Yes, Captain; but with this acknowledgment, 120
That God fought for us.

    Flu. Yes, my conscience, he did us great good.

    King. Do we all holy rites.
Let there be sung "Non nobis" and "Te Deum,"
The dead with charity enclosed in clay,   125
And then to Calais; and to England then;
Where ne'er from France arrived more happy men.
                                     Exeunt.

THE LIFE OF
KING HENRY
THE FIFTH

ACT V

Cho. V. The Chorus describes the triumphant return of King Henry and his men to London, but relates that he then returned to France to settle the terms of peace with the French King.

▬▬▬▬▬▬▬▬▬▬▬▬▬▬▬▬

3-4. admit the excuse/ Of: that is, be tolerant of the acting company's inability to show everything that happened.

10. Pales in: encloses, as does a fence.

13. whiffler: an official who cleared the way for a royal or municipal procession.

19. His bruised helmet and his bended sword: i.e., the visible proofs of his part in the battle.

ACT V

Enter *Chorus.*

Vouchsafe to those that have not read the story
That I may prompt them; and of such as have,
I humbly pray them to admit the excuse
Of time, of numbers, and due course of things
Which cannot in their huge and proper life   5
Be here presented. Now we bear the King
Toward Calais. Grant him there. There seen,
Heave him away upon your winged thoughts
Athwart the sea. Behold, the English beach
Pales in the flood with men, wives, and boys,   10
Whose shouts and claps outvoice the deep-mouthed
    sea,
Which, like a mighty whiffler fore the King,
Seems to prepare his way. So let him land,
And solemnly see him set on to London.   15
So swift a pace hath thought that even now
You may imagine him upon Blackheath;
Where that his lords desire him to have borne
His bruised helmet and his bended sword
Before him through the city. He forbids it,   20

22-3. Giving full trophy, signal, and ostent/ Quite from himself to God: disdaining the display of any symbols of victory because to God alone could the victory be attributed.

30. loving likelihood: a possibility eagerly desired.

31. the general of our gracious Empress: Robert Devereux, Earl of Essex, who had been commissioned to settle the revolt in Ireland. Actually, his conduct there was a disappointment to the Queen and ultimately led to his complete disgrace and the rebellion that ended with his execution in 1601.

33. broached: spitted.

37-8. As yet the lamentation of the French/ Invites the King of England's stay at home: that is, the French are still bowed down by their defeat and there is no need for the English King to hurry back.

39. Emperor: The Emperor of the Holy Roman Empire, Sigismund, who visited England on May 1, 1416.

40. order: arrange.

43-4. myself have played/ The interim: i.e., the Chorus has informed the audience of the intervening events not revealed in the action.

45. brook abridgment: allow us to abridge these happenings.

Being free from vainness and self-glorious pride;
Giving full trophy, signal, and ostent
Quite from himself to God. But now behold,
In the quick forge and working house of thought,
How London doth pour out her citizens!　　　　25
The Mayor and all his brethren in best sort—
Like to the senators of the antique Rome,
With the plebeians swarming at their heels—
Go forth and fetch their conqu'ring Cæsar in;
As, by a lower but by loving likelihood,　　　　30
Were now the general of our gracious Empress
(As in good time he may) from Ireland coming,
Bringing rebellion broached on his sword,
How many would the peaceful city quit
To welcome him! Much more, and much more cause, 35
Did they this Harry. Now in London place him
(As yet the lamentation of the French
Invites the King of England's stay at home;
The Emperor's coming in behalf of France
To order peace between them) and omit　　　　40
All the occurrences, whatever chanced,
Till Harry's back-return again to France.
There must we bring him; and myself have played
The interim, by rememb'ring you 'tis past.
Then brook abridgment; and your eyes advance,　45
After your thoughts, straight back again to France.
　　　　　　　　　　　　　　　　　　Exit.

V. [i.] Fluellen lies in wait for Pistol because the latter has made fun of him for wearing the Welsh leek. Though Pistol blusters, Fluellen cudgels him and forces him to eat the leek. Pistol swears a horrible revenge, but alone he muses on his sad lot: his wife is dead and no one waits for him at home; the only future he has to look forward to is a hand-to-mouth existence by petty thievery.

5. **scauld:** scurvy; i.e., scabrous.

19. **bedlam:** lunatic. **Bedlam** is a corruption of Bethlehem, the name of a hospital for the insane in London.

20. **Trojan:** in popular Elizabethan parlance, a term for a roistering fellow.

21. **fold up Parca's fatal web:** i.e., kill you. The classical Fates were known as the Parcae, and were pictured as three women, one of whom spun the web of human life, while another decided its length and the third cut it.

22. **qualmish:** queasy.

[Scene I. France. The English camp.]

Enter *Fluellen* and *Gower.*

Gow. Nay, that's right. But why wear you your leek
today? Saint Davy's day is past.

Flu. There is occasions and causes why and wherefore in all things. I will tell you ass my friend, Captain
Gower. The rascally, scauld, beggarly, lousy, pragging   5
knave, Pistol—which you and yourself and all the
world know to be no petter than a fellow, look you
now, of no merits—he is come to me and prings me
pread and salt yesterday, look you, and bid me eat my
leek. It was in a place where I could not breed no   10
contention with him; but I will be so bold as to wear
it in my cap till I see him once again, and then I will
tell him a little piece of my desires.

Enter *Pistol.*

Gow. Why, here he comes, swelling like a turkey
cock.   15

Flu. 'Tis no matter for his swellings nor his turkey
cocks. God pless you, Aunchient Pistol! you scurvy,
lousy knave, God pless you!

Pist. Ha! art thou bedlam? Dost thou thirst, base
Trojan,   20
To have me fold up Parca's fatal web?
Hence! I am qualmish at the smell of leek.

Flu. I peseech you heartily, scurvy, lousy knave,

29. **Cadwallader:** the last king of Wales. Goats were associated in English minds with Wales, and Pistol is deliberately being as insulting as possible; this is not a reference to any historical connection between King Cadwallader and goats.

36. **mountain-squire:** that is, a man whose property consists only of mountain lands of no value.

37. **a squire of low degree:** i.e., Fluellen threatens to take Pistol down a peg. The phrase was also the title of a medieval romance.

39. **astonished:** stunned.

42-3. **green:** fresh, new; **coxcomb:** head.

at my desires, and my requests, and my petitions, to
eat, look you, this leek. Because, look you, you do not   25
love it, nor your affections and your appetites and
your disgestions doo's not agree with it, I would desire
you to eat it.

Pist. Not for Cadwallader and all his goats.

Flu. There is one goat for you. (*Strikes him.*) Will   30
you be so good, scauld knave, as eat it?

Pist. Base Trojan, thou shalt die!

Flu. You say very true, scauld knave, when God's
will is. I will desire you to live in the meantime, and
eat your victuals. Come, there is sauce for it. [*Strikes*   35
him.] You called me yesterday mountain-squire; but I
will make you today a squire of low degree. I pray
you fall to. If you can mock a leek, you can eat a leek.

Gow. Enough, Captain. You have astonished him.

Flu. I say I will make him eat some part of my leek   40
or I will peat his pate four days.—Bite, I pray you. It
is good for your green wound and your ploody coxcomb.

Pist. Must I bite?

Flu. Yes, certainly, and out of doubt, and out of   45
question too, and ambiguities.

Pist. By this leek, I will most horribly revenge! I
eat, and yet, I swear—

Flu. Eat, I pray you. Will you have some more
sauce to your leek? There is not enough leek to swear   50
by.

Pist. Quiet thy cudgel. Thou dost see I eat.

Flu. Much good do you, scauld knave, heartily.
Nay, pray you throw none away. The skin is good for

63. **in earnest of revenge:** i.e., in part payment
of the revenge you owe me. See **earnest,** [II. ii.]
182.

70-1. **upon an honorable respect:** i.e, for an
honorable reason.

73-4. **gleeking and galling:** mocking and jeer-
ing.

75. **garb:** style.

79. **huswife:** hussy, wanton.

84. **bawd:** procurer.

your broken coxcomb. When you take occasions to see   55
leeks hereafter, I pray you mock at 'em; that is all.

Pist. Good.

Flu. Ay, leeks is good. Hold you, there is a groat
to heal your pate.

Pist. Me a groat?   60

Flu. Yes, verily and in truth, you shall take it; or I
have another leek in my pocket, which you shall eat.

Pist. I take thy groat in earnest of revenge.

Flu. If I owe you anything, I will pay you in
cudgels. You shall be a woodmonger and buy nothing   65
of me but cudgels. God be wi' you, and keep you, and
heal your pate.   *Exit.*

Pist. All hell shall stir for this!

Gow. Go, go. You are a counterfeit cowardly knave.
Will you mock at an ancient tradition, begun upon an   70
honorable respect and worn as a memorable trophy of
predeceased valor, and dare not avouch in your deeds
any of your words? I have seen you gleeking and
galling at this gentleman twice or thrice. You thought,
because he could not speak English in the native garb, 75
he could not therefore handle an English cudgel. You
find it otherwise; and henceforth let a Welsh correction teach you a good English condition. Fare ye well.
                                        Exit.

Pist. Doth Fortune play the huswife with me now?
News have I, that my Nell is dead i' the spital   80
Of malady of France;
And there my rendezvous is quite cut off.
Old I do wax, and from my weary limbs
Honor is cudgeled. Well, bawd will I turn,

85. **something:** somewhat; **cutpurse:** pickpocket.
88. **Gallia wars:** French wars.

▬▬▬▬▬▬▬▬▬▬▬▬▬▬▬▬▬▬▬▬▬▬

V. [ii.] King Henry and his lords meet with the French King and Queen, the Duke of Burgundy, and other advisers to agree on terms of peace. One of Henry's conditions is the hand of the Princess Katherine, and he takes the earliest opportunity of pressing his personal suit for her love. The Princess is shy but finally gives her consent to marry him if it is her father's will.

The French King and his counselors declare their acceptance of the terms submitted by King Henry, even including Henry's stipulations that he be acknowledged as heir to the throne of France and be married to the Princess.

▬▬▬▬▬▬▬▬▬▬▬▬▬▬▬▬▬▬

1-2. **Peace to this meeting, wherefore we are met:** i.e., the meeting was for the purpose of settling the terms of peace.

And something lean to cutpurse of quick hand.   85
To England will I steal, and there I'll steal;
And patches will I get unto these cudgeled scars
And swear I got them in the Gallia wars.

Exit.

[Scene II. France. The King's Palace.]

Enter, *at one door,* King Henry, Exeter, Bedford,
[*Gloucester,*] Warwick, [*Westmoreland,*] *and other
Lords; at another,* Queen Isabel, *the* [*French*] King,
the Duke of Burgundy, [*the* Princess Katherine,
Alice,] *and other* French.

King H. Peace to this meeting, wherefore we are
    met!
Unto our brother France and to our sister
Health and fair time of day. Joy and good wishes
To our most fair and princely cousin Katherine.   5
And as a branch and member of this royalty,
By whom this great assembly is contrived,
We do salute you, Duke of Burgundy.
And, princes French, and peers, health to you all!
    France. Right joyous are we to behold your face,   10
Most worthy brother England. Fairly met.
So are you, princes English, every one.
    Queen. So happy be the issue, brother England,
Of this good day and of this gracious meeting
As we are now glad to behold your eyes—   15
Your eyes which hitherto have borne in them,

17. **met them in their bent:** came into their line of vision; crossed the path of their aim.

18. **balls:** eyeballs and cannonballs; **basilisks:** a type of cannon and also a fabulous monster possessed of a murderous glance.

24. **on equal love:** based on equal love for both of you.

33. **congreeted:** greeted each other.

42. **it:** its, an old form of the genitive.

44. **even-pleached:** with the edges trained back to present an even top layer of the branches.

46. **fallow leas:** unplowed meadows.

47. **darnel:** a weed particularly infesting fields of grain; **rank:** luxuriant; **fumitory:** another weed.

A basilisk.
From Conrad Lycosthenes, *Prodigiorum* (1557).

Against the French that met them in their bent,
The fatal balls of murdering basilisks.
The venom of such looks, we fairly hope,
Have lost their quality, and that this day   20
Shall change all griefs and quarrels into love.
   King H. To cry amen to that, thus we appear.
   Queen. You English princes all, I do salute you.
   Burg. My duty to you both, on equal love,
Great Kings of France and England! That I have   25
    labored
With all my wits, my pains, and strong endeavors
To bring your most imperial Majesties
Unto this bar and royal interview,
Your mightiness on both parts best can witness.   30
Since, then, my office hath so far prevailed
That, face to face and royal eye to eye,
You have congreeted, let it not disgrace me
If I demand, before this royal view,
What rub or what impediment there is   35
Why that the naked, poor, and mangled Peace,
Dear nurse of arts, plenty, and joyful births,
Should not, in this best garden of the world,
Our fertile France, put up her lovely visage.
Alas, she hath from France too long been chased!   40
And all her husbandry doth lie on heaps,
Corrupting in it own fertility.
Her vine, the merry cheerer of the heart,
Unpruned dies; her hedges even-pleached,
Like prisoners wildly overgrown with hair,   45
Put forth disordered twigs; her fallow leas
The darnel, hemlock, and rank fumitory

48. **coulter:** the blade of the plow.

49. **deracinate:** tear up by the roots and hence destroy.

50. **erst:** formerly.

53. **Conceives by idleness:** i.e., the uncultivated meadow produces unprofitable weeds; **nothing teems:** produces nothing.

54. **kecksies:** dry weed stalks.

63. **diffused:** disordered.

65. **favor:** fine appearance.

67. **let:** hindrance.

70. **would:** i.e., would like, desire.

75. **tenures:** general terms.

Doth root upon, while that the coulter rusts
That should deracinate such savagery.
The even mead, that erst brought sweetly forth   50
The freckled cowslip, burnet, and green clover,
Wanting the scythe, all uncorrected, rank,
Conceives by idleness and nothing teems
But hateful docks, rough thistles, kecksies, burrs,
Losing both beauty and utility.   55
And all our vineyards, fallows, meads, and hedges,
Defective in their natures, grow to wildness,
Even so our houses and ourselves and children
Have lost, or do not learn for want of time,
The sciences that should become our country;   60
But grow like savages—as soldiers will,
That nothing do but meditate on blood—
To swearing and stern looks, diffused attire,
And everything that seems unnatural.
Which to reduce into our former favor   65
You are assembled; and my speech entreats
That I may know the let why gentle Peace
Should not expel these inconveniences
And bless us with her former qualities.

    King H. If, Duke of Burgundy, you would the 70
      peace
Whose want gives growth to the imperfections
Which you have cited, you must buy that peace
With full accord to all our just demands;
Whose tenures and particular effects   75
You have, enscheduled briefly, in your hands.

    Burg. The King hath heard them; to the which as
      yet

82. **cursitory:** cursory, hasty.

83. **Pleaseth your Grace:** if it please your Grace.

84. **presently:** at once.

87. **Pass our accept and peremptory answer:** give our final answer as to what is acceptable to us.

95. **consign:** i.e., set my seal, agree.

98. **Happily:** haply, perhaps.

99. **When articles too nicely urged be stood on:** when points only mentioned out of a punctilious concern with detail are insisted upon.

There is no answer made.

 King H.   Well then, the peace, 80
Which you before so urged, lies in his answer.

 France. I have but with a cursitory eye
O'erglanced the articles. Pleaseth your Grace
To appoint some of your Council presently
To sit with us once more, with better heed 85
To resurvey them, we will suddenly
Pass our accept and peremptory answer.

 King H. Brother, we shall. Go, uncle Exeter,
And brother Clarence, and you, brother Gloucester,
Warwick, and Huntingdon—go with the King; 90
And take with you free power to ratify,
Augment, or alter, as your wisdoms best
Shall see advantageable for our dignity,
Anything in or out of our demands;
And we'll consign thereto. Will you, fair sister, 95
Go with the princes or stay here with us?

 Queen. Our gracious brother, I will go with them.
Happily a woman's voice may do some good
When articles too nicely urged be stood on.

 King H. Yet leave our cousin Katherine here with 100
  us.
She is our capital demand, comprised
Within the forerank of our articles.

 Queen. She hath good leave.

    Exeunt. Manent King Henry, Katherine,
      and the Gentlewoman [*Alice*].

 King H.   Fair Katherine, and most fair! 105
Will you vouchsafe to teach a soldier terms

130. The Princess is the better Englishwoman:
i.e., because she prefers plain speech and recognizes
flattery for what it is. Henry is probably doing some
"wishful thinking" in view of his disclaimer of any
ability for flowery compliment.

Such as will enter at a lady's ear
And plead his love suit to her gentle heart?

Kath. Your Majesty shall mock at me. I cannot
speak your England.   110

King H. O fair Katherine, if you will love me
soundly with your French heart, I will be glad to hear
you confess it brokenly with your English tongue. Do
you like me, Kate?

Kath. Pardonnez-moi, I cannot tell wat is "like me." 115

King H. An angel is like you, Kate, and you are
like an angel.

Kath. Que dit-il? Que je suis semblable à les
anges?

Alice. Oui, vraiment, sauf votre grâce, ainsi dit- 120
il.

King H. I said so, dear Katherine, and I must not
blush to affirm it.

Kath. O bon Dieu! les langues des hommes sont
pleines de tromperies.   125

King H. What says she, fair one? that the tongues
of men are full of deceits?

Alice. Oui, dat de tongues of de mans is be full of
deceits. Dat is de Princesse.

King H. The Princess is the better Englishwoman. 130
I' faith, Kate, my wooing is fit for thy understanding.
I am glad thou canst speak no better English; for if
thou couldst, thou wouldst find me such a plain king
that thou wouldst think I had sold my farm to buy
my crown. I know no ways to mince it in love but 135
directly to say "I love you." Then, if you urge me
farther than to say, "Do you in faith?" I wear out my

142. **you undid me:** i.e., you would undo me.

144-45. **I have no strength in measure, yet a reasonable measure in strength:** I am not strong at treading dance measures but I have a fair share of physical strength.

147-48. **under the correction of bragging be it spoken:** though I may risk being accused of bragging in saying so.

149. **buffet:** box.

151. **jackanapes:** a tame ape or monkey. Monkeys trained to ride horseback were sometimes a feature of Elizabethan "vaudeville" acts at fairs and the like.

152. **look greenly:** make sheep's eyes like a callow, lovesick youth.

156. **not worth sunburning:** that is, so far from handsome at best that sunburn would little harm it.

158. **let thine eye be thy cook:** i.e., let your eye dress me to suit your taste, as a cook might present a dish with fancy trimmings to disguise its plainness.

163. **uncoined constancy:** constancy never made current; i.e., inexperienced in love.

suit. Give me your answer; i' faith, do! and so clap
hands and a bargain. How say you, lady?

Kath. Sauf votre honneur, me understand well.   140

King H. Marry, if you would put me to verses or
to dance for your sake, Kate, why, you undid me.
For the one I have neither words nor measure; and
for the other I have no strength in measure, yet a
reasonable measure in strength. If I could win a lady 145
at leapfrog, or by vaulting into my saddle with my
armor on my back, under the correction of bragging
be it spoken, I should quickly leap into a wife. Or if·
I might buffet for my love, or bound my horse for her
favors, I could lay on like a butcher and sit like a 150
jackanapes, never off. But, before God, Kate, I cannot look greenly nor gasp out my eloquence, nor I
have no cunning in protestation; only downright
oaths, which I never use till urged, nor never break
for urging. If thou canst love a fellow of this temper, 155
Kate, whose face is not worth sunburning, that never
looks in his glass for love of anything he sees there,
let thine eye be thy cook. I speak to thee plain soldier. If thou canst love me for this, take me; if not,
to say to thee that I shall die, is true—but for thy 160
love, by the Lord, no; yet I love thee too. And while
thou livest, dear Kate, take a fellow of plain and
uncoined constancy; for he perforce must do thee
right, because he hath not the gift to woo in other
places. For these fellows of infinite tongue that can 165
rhyme themselves into ladies' favors, they do always
reason themselves out again. What! A speaker is but
a prater; a rhyme is but a ballad. A good leg will

193. Saint Denis: the patron saint of France.

fall, a straight back will stoop, a black beard will
turn white, a curled pate will grow bald, a fair face 170
will wither, a full eye will wax hollow; but a good
heart, Kate, is the sun and the moon; or rather, the
sun, and not the moon, for it shines bright and never
changes, but keeps his course truly. If thou would
have such a one, take me; and take me, take a sol- 175
dier; take a soldier, take a king. And what sayst thou
then to my love? Speak, my fair—and fairly, I pray
thee.

Kath. Is it possible dat I sould love de enemy of
France? 180

King H. No, it is not possible you should love the
enemy of France, Kate; but in loving me you should
love the friend of France; for I love France so well
that I will not part with a village of it—I will have it
all mine. And, Kate, when France is mine and I am 185
yours, then yours is France and you are mine.

Kath. I cannot tell wat is dat.

King H. No, Kate? I will tell thee in French; which
I am sure will hang upon my tongue like a new-
married wife about her husband's neck, hardly to 190
be shook off. Quand j'ai la possession de France, et
quand vous avez la possession de moi (let me see,
what then? Saint Denis be my speed!), donc votre
est France et vous êtes mienne. It is as easy for me,
Kate, to conquer the kingdom as to speak so much 195
more French. I shall never move thee in French, unless it be to laugh at me.

Kath. Sauf votre honneur, le Français que vous
parlez, il est meilleur que l'Anglais lequel je parle.

201. **truly-falsely:** sincerely if inaccurately.

202. **much at one:** about equal.

208. **closet:** private chamber.

214-15. **with scambling:** as the result of war; see I. i. 4.

225. **moiety:** half.

226-27. **la plus belle Katherine du monde, mon très-cher et divin déesse:** the most beautiful Katherine in the world, my most dear and divine goddess.

228. **fausse:** false.

King H. No, faith, is't not, Kate. But thy speak- 200
ing of my tongue, and I thine, most truly-falsely,
must needs be granted to be much at one. But, Kate,
dost thou understand thus much English? Canst thou
love me?

Kath. I cannot tell. 205

King H. Can any of your neighbors tell, Kate? I'll
ask them. Come, I know thou lovest me; and at night
when you come into your closet, you'll question this
gentlewoman about me; and I know, Kate, you will
to her dispraise those parts in me that you love with 210
your heart; but, good Kate, mock me mercifully, the
rather, gentle Princess, because I love thee cruelly.
If ever thou beest mine, Kate—as I have a saving
faith within me tells me thou shalt—I get thee with
scambling, and thou must therefore needs prove a 215
good soldier-breeder. Shall not thou and I, between
Saint Denis and Saint George, compound a boy, half
French, half English, that shall go to Constantinople
and take the Turk by the beard? Shall we not? What
sayst thou, my fair flower-de-luce? 220

Kath. I do not know dat.

King H. No; 'tis hereafter to know, but now to
promise. Do but now promise, Kate, you will endeavor for your French part of such a boy; and for
my English moiety take the word of a king and a 225
bachelor. How answer you, la plus belle Katherine
du monde, mon très-cher et divin déesse?

Kath. Your Majestee ave fausse French enough to
deceive de most sage demoiselle dat is en France.

King H. Now, fie upon my false French! By mine 230

232. **my blood:** i.e., the strength of my own eagerness.

234. **untempering:** unpersuasive; see [II. ii.] 129.

235. **beshrew:** curse.

237. **stubborn:** rough, harsh.

240. **layer-up:** preserver.

254-55. **broken music:** music played by varied instruments, instead of by a set of like instruments such as viols or recorders.

honor in true English, I love thee, Kate; by which
honor I dare not swear thou lovest me; yet my blood
begins to flatter me that thou dost, notwithstanding
the poor and untempering effect of my visage. Now
beshrew my father's ambition! He was thinking of 235
civil wars when he got me; therefore was I created
with a stubborn outside, with an aspect of iron, that,
when I come to woo ladies, I fright them. But in
faith, Kate, the elder I wax, the better I shall appear.
My comfort is, that old age, that ill layer up of 240
beauty, can do no more spoil upon my face. Thou
hast me, if thou hast me, at the worst; and thou shalt
wear me, if thou wear me, better and better; and
therefore tell me, most fair Katherine, will you
have me? Put off your maiden blushes; avouch 245
the thoughts of your heart with the looks of an
empress; take me by the hand, and say "Harry of
England, I am thine!" which word thou shalt no
sooner bless mine ear withal but I will tell thee
aloud "England is thine, Ireland is thine, France 250
is thine, and Henry Plantagenet is thine"; who,
though I speak it before his face, if he be not fellow with the best king, thou shalt find the best
king of good fellows. Come, your answer in broken
music! for thy voice is music and thy English broken, 255
therefore, queen of all Katherines, break thy mind
to me in broken English. Wilt thou have me?

Kath. Dat is as it sall please de roi mon père.

King H. Nay, it will please him well, Kate. It shall
please him, Kate.   260

Kath. Den it sall also content me.

264-68. **Laissez . . . seigneur:** let go, my Lord, let go, let go. My faith, I do not at all wish that you should abase your greatness in kissing the hand of one of your Lordship's unworthy servants. Excuse me, I beg of you, my most powerful Lord.

280. **nice:** observant of polite niceties; see **nicely,** l. 99.

282. **list:** enclosure, barrier; possibly with a pun on another meaning: the border of a fabric.

283-84. **follows our places:** attends our stations in life.

King H. Upon that I kiss your hand and I call you
my queen.

Kath. Laissez, mon seigneur, laissez, laissez! Ma
foi, je ne veux point que vous abaissiez votre gran-   265
deur en baisant la main d'une de votre seigneurie
indigne serviteur. Excusez-moi, je vous supplie, mon
très-puissant seigneur.

King H. Then I will kiss your lips, Kate.

Kath. Les dames et demoiselles pour être baisées   270
devant leur noces, il n'est pas la coutume de France.

King H. Madam my interpreter, what says she?

Alice. Dat it is not be de fashon pour de ladies of
France—I cannot tell vat is "baiser" en Anglish.

King H. To kiss.   275

Alice. Your Majestee entendre bettre que moi.

King H. It is not a fashion for the maids in France
to kiss before they are married, would she say?

Alice. Oui, vraiment.

King H. O Kate, nice customs curtsy to great   280
kings. Dear Kate, you and I cannot be confined within the weak list of a country's fashion. We are the
makers of manners, Kate; and the liberty that follows our places stops the mouth of all find-faults, as
I will do yours for upholding the nice fashion of your 285
country in denying me a kiss. Therefore patiently,
and yielding. [*Kisses her.*] You have witchcraft in
your lips, Kate. There is more eloquence in a sugar
touch of them than in the tongues of the French
Council, and they should sooner persuade Harry of   290
England than a general petition of monarchs. Here
comes your father.

298-99. **condition:** disposition.

306. **blind:** uncontrollable; see [III. iii.] 34.

320-21. **Bartholomew-tide:** August 24, St. Bartholomew's Day, when flies become sluggish.

Enter the *French Power* and the *English Lords.*

Burg. God save your Majesty! My royal cousin,
Teach you our princess English?

King H. I would have her learn, my fair cousin, 295
how perfectly I love her, and that is good English.

Burg. Is she not apt?

King H. Our tongue is rough, coz, and my condition is not smooth; so that, having neither the voice
nor the heart of flattery about me, I cannot so con- 300
jure up the spirit of love in her that he will appear
in his true likeness.

Burg. Pardon the frankness of my mirth if I answer you for that. If you would conjure in her, you
must make a circle; if conjure up love in her in his 305
true likeness, he must appear naked and blind. Can
you blame her then, being a maid yet rosed over
with the virgin crimson of modesty, if she deny the
appearance of a naked blind boy in her naked seeing
self? It were, my lord, a hard condition for a maid 310
to consign to.

King H. Yet they do wink and yield, as love is
blind and enforces.

Burg. They are then excused, my lord, when they
see not what they do. 315

King H. Then, good my lord, teach your cousin to
consent winking.

Burg. I will wink on her to consent, my lord, if you
will teach her to know my meaning; for maids well
summered and warm kept are like flies at Bartholo- 320

324. **This moral ties me over to:** this example binds me to; i.e., I shall have to wait for warm weather to set in.

332. **perspectively:** i.e., through a "perspective glass," which presents a distortion of reality.

338-40. **wait on her:** attend her; that is, accompany her as part of her dowry; **stood in the way for my wish:** interfered with my securing the cities referred to; **my will:** that is, his desire for Katherine herself.

345. **According to their firm proposed natures:** in exact accordance with the strict letter of the stipulations.

346. **subscribed:** agreed to.

350-51. **Notre très-cher fils Henri, Roi d'-Angleterre, héritier de France:** our most dear son Henry, King of England, heir to the throne of France.

mew-tide, blind, though they have their eyes; and
then they will endure handling which before would
not abide looking on.

King H. This moral ties me over to time and a hot
summer; and so I shall catch the fly, your cousin, in 325
the latter end, and she must be blind too.

Burg. As love is, my lord, before it loves.

King H. It is so; and you may, some of you, thank
love for my blindness, who cannot see many a fair
French city for one fair French maid that stands in 330
my way.

France. Yes, my lord, you see them perspectively
—the cities turned into a maid; for they are all girdled
with maiden walls that war hath never ent'red.

King H. Shall Kate be my wife?   335

France. So please you.

King H. I am content, so the maiden cities you
talk of may wait on her. So the maid that stood in
the way for my wish shall show me the way to my
will.   340

France. We have consented to all terms of reason.

King H. Is't so, my lords of England?

West. The King hath granted every article:
His daughter first; and in sequel, all,
According to their firm proposed natures.   345

Exe. Only he hath not yet subscribed this: Where
your Majesty demands that the King of France, having any occasion to write for matter of grant, shall
name your Highness in this form and with this addition, in French, "Notre très-cher fils Henri, Roi 350
d'Angleterre, héritier de France"; and thus in Latin,

354-55. **so denied/ But your request shall make me let it pass:** i.e., refused so irrevocably that your mere request that it be granted will not influence me to accept it.

365. **neighborhood:** neighborliness.

376. **office:** action; **fell:** cruel.

378. **paction:** concord.

From Brute to King Iames.

Anno Dom. 1422

Henry the fixt.

THis Infant Prince scarce being nine months old,
The Realms of *France* & *England* he did hold:
But he vncapable, thtought want of yeeres,
Was ouergouern'd, by mifgouern'd Peeres.
Now *Yorke* and *Lancaster*, with bloudy wars
Both wound this kingdom, with deep deadly scars
Whilst this good King by *Yorke* oppos'd; depos'd,
Expos'd to dangers is Captin'd, inclos'd,
His Queene exilde, his Son, and many friends,
Fled, murdred, flaughter'd; laftly fate contends,
To Crowne him once againe, who then at laft
VVas murdered, thirty nine yeeres being paft.

Anno Dom. 1460

King Henry VI.
From John Taylor, *A Memorial of All the English Monarchs*
(1622).

122

"Praecarissimus filius noster Henricus, Rex Angliae
et haeres Franciae."

France. Nor this I have not, brother, so denied
But your request shall make me let it pass.   355

King H. I pray you then, in love and dear alliance,
Let that one article rank with the rest,
And thereupon give me your daughter.

France. Take her, fair son, and from her blood
raise up   360
Issue to me, that the contending kingdoms
Of France and England, whose very shores look pale
With envy of each other's happiness,
May cease their hatred; and this dear conjunction
Plant neighborhood and Christianlike accord   365
In their sweet bosoms, that never war advance
His bleeding sword 'twixt England and fair France.

Lords. Amen!

King H. Now, welcome, Kate; and bear me witness all   370
That here I kiss her as my sovereign queen.

                                        Flourish.

Queen. God, the best maker of all marriages,
Combine your hearts in one, your realms in one!
As man and wife, being two, are one in love,
So be there 'twixt your kingdoms such a spousal   375
That never may ill office, or fell jealousy,
Which troubles oft the bed of blessed marriage,
Thrust in between the paction of these kingdoms
To make divorce of their incorporate league;
That English may as French, French Englishmen, 380-
Receive each other! God speak this Amen!

2. **bending:** humble; bowing to the audience in the hope of a favorable reception.

4. **by starts:** by presenting in bits and pieces instead of as a full and connected story.

5. **Small time:** a reference to Henry's early death, at the age of thirty-five.

13. **Which oft our stage hath shown; and for their sake:** i.e., Shakespeare's *Henry VI*, in three parts, had already been popular, and the author pleads for a charitable reaction to the foregoing play in recognition of the fact.

All. Amen!

King H. Prepare we for our marriage; on which
   day,
My Lord of Burgundy, we'll take your oath, 385
And all the peers', for surety of our leagues.
Then shall I swear to Kate, and you to me,
And may our oaths well kept and prosp'rous be!

Sennet. Exeunt.

[Epilogue]

Enter Chorus.

Thus far, with rough and all-unable pen,
   Our bending author hath pursued the story,
In little room confining mighty men,
   Mangling by starts the full course of their glory.
Small time; but in that small, most greatly lived 5
   This Star of England. Fortune made his sword;
By which the world's best garden he achieved,
   And of it left his son imperial lord.
Henry the Sixth, in infant bands crowned King
   Of France and England, did this king succeed; 10
Whose state so many had the managing
   That they lost France and made his England bleed;
Which oft our stage hath shown; and for their sake
In your fair minds let this acceptance take.

[Exit.]

Famous Lines and Phrases

For government, though high, and low, and lower,
Put into parts, doth keep in one consent,
Congreeing in a full and natural close,
Like music.   [*Exeter*—I. ii. 186-89]

When we have matched our rackets to these balls,
We will in France (by God's grace) play a set
Shall strike his father's crown into the hazard.
                    [*Henry*—I. ii. 273-75]

. . . the mirror of all Christian kings   [*Chorus*—II. 6]

For after I saw him fumble with the sheets, and play
    with flowers, and smile upon his finger's end, I
    knew there was but one way; for his nose was as
    sharp as a pen, and 'a babbled of green fields.
                    [*Hostess*—II. iii. 13-7]

The kindred of him hath been fleshed upon us;
And he is bred out of that bloody strain
That haunted us in our familiar paths.
                    [*French King*—II. iv. 54-6]

Once more unto the breach, dear friends, once more;
Or close the wall up with our English dead!
In peace there's nothing so becomes a man
As modest stillness and humility . . . [*Henry*—III. i. 1 ff.]

I would give all my fame for a pot of ale
and safety.   [*Boy*—III. ii. 13-4]

. . . mean and gentle all
Behold, as may unworthiness define,
A little touch of Harry in the night.

[*Chorus*—IV. 45-7]

. . . What infinite heart's-ease
Must kings neglect that private men enjoy!
And what have kings that privates have not too,
Save ceremony, save general ceremony? . . .

[*Henry*—IV. i. 240 ff.]

. . . if it be a sin to covet honor,
I am the most offending soul alive. [*Henry*—IV. iii. 32-3]

We few, we happy few, we band of brothers . . .

[*Henry*—IV. iii. 64]

Small time; but in that small, most greatly lived
This Star of England. . . .   [*Epilogue*—5-6]